Ruby Tuesday

An Eddie Dancer Mystery

Mike Harrison

ECW Press

Published by ECW PRESS
2120 Queen Street East, Suite 200, Toronto, Ontario, Canada M4E 1E2

LIBRARY AND ARCHIVES CANADA CATALOGUING IN PUBLICATION

Harrison, Mike (Mike S.), 1945–
Ruby Tuesday / Mike Harrison

(An Eddie Dancer mystery)
ISBN-13: 978-1-55022-792-5

I. Title. II. Series: Harrison, Mike (Mike S.), 1945– Eddie Dancer Mystery

PS8615.A749R82 2007   C813'.6   C2007-903488-8

Cover and Text Design: Tania Craan
Cover Image: G. Biss / Masterfile
Typesetting: Mary Bowness
Production: Rachel Brooks
Printing: Friesens

This book is set in Sabon and Bubba Love

The publication of *Ruby Tuesday* has been generously supported by the Canada
Council for the Arts, which last year invested $20.1 million in writing and publishing
throughout Canada, by the Ontario Arts Council, by the Government of Ontario
through Ontario Book Publishing Tax Credit, and the Government of Canada through
the Book Publishing Industry Development Program (BPIDP).

Canada Council   Conseil des Arts   ONTARIO ARTS COUNCIL
for the Arts   du Canada   CONSEIL DES ARTS DE L'ONTARIO

DISTRIBUTION
CANADA: Jaguar Book Group, 100 Armstrong Ave.,
Georgetown, ON L7G 5S4
UNITED STATES: Independent Publishers Group,
814 North Franklin St., Chicago, IL 60610

PRINTED AND BOUND IN CANADA

ECW PRESS
ecwpress.com

For all the folks
In Okotoks

~

Special thanks go to my wife, Jan, to Alec, Annalisa and the lovely new Emilea and to Gavin and Sarin for their continued love and support.

Special thanks also to my reading group, Tricia Coles, Margaret Fergusson, Andrew Fulcher, Janet Klippenstein, Kelly McLachlan and Chris Podesky, for burning the midnight oil.

Also thanks to the real Nicole Laurin who generously donated an enormous amount of money to the Calgary Real Estate Board Charitable Foundation and allowed me to use her name as a character in this book. Her kind-hearted donation went towards the Crestwood HOME AT LAST Campaign for Affordable Housing. Good on yer, Nicole.

And finally, major thanks are overdue to Edna Barker who has diligently edited all three of the Eddie Dancer mysteries with such patience, fortitude and skill, she could undoubtedly write the next three without me.

Chapter One

I WASN'T THERE, BUT THIS is what happened to Paul Miller on the second Thursday in April, as told to me by Valerie, his wife of twenty-seven years.

She came to see me in my office, unannounced, one bright spring morning in early May. I was sitting at my desk, feet up, hands locked behind my head, balancing body and soul and wrestling with seventeen across in the *Calgary Herald*'s crossword — a five-letter word meaning "to turn inside out."

I swivelled towards the door as it squeaked open. She was unannounced because I have no receptionist. No secretary. No pretty young thing to proclaim the arrival of potential new clients. I save on a secretary's salary by not oiling the door hinges. People just walk in off the street and tell me their life stories.

Or at least, the nasty bits.

And Valerie Miller's nasty bits were as nasty as anyone else's.

No more, no less.

But it was early days and there was plenty of time for things to get worse. And they did. Much worse. But I'm getting ahead of the game.

She paused a moment, unimpressed by my feet on the desk. I could tell patience wasn't high on her list of virtues.

"I need a five-letter word meaning 'to turn inside out,'" I told her.

She never missed a beat.

"My life."

"One too many letters."

And one too many words, but she wasn't in the mood to stand corrected a second time.

"Story of my life," she said. She slumped in the chair across from my desk and pulled out a pack of cigarettes. "Y'mind?"

"Yup."

She paused again, the unlit cigarette clamped between full lips.

"You're kidding?" she said, out the side of her mouth.

"Nope."

She snatched the cigarette back and crushed it into the carton.

"Jesus H. Christ. Nobody told me you were goody two-shoes."

She didn't seem to expect an answer so I just gave her my goody two-shoes smile.

"You *are* Eddie Dancer, aren't you?" she asked emphatically.

"Yup," I said emphatically back.

"Eddie Dancer, *the* private detective?" she said.

"Uh-huh."

Some days you just can't shut me up.

"You don't seem very —" she waved a hand in the air "— detectively."

"How about I shoot a hole in your sunroof? In the Lexus?"

That got her attention.

"How'd you know what I drive?"

"I saw you pull in."

She glanced out the window at my million-dollar view of the parking lot and shrugged.

Mystery solved.

"You're sure about the cigarette thing?" she asked.

"Golden rule."

"Crap. Okay, where do I start?"

"Depends. How long can you go without one?"

"Without bitchin' you to death?"

"Preferably."

She drummed her fingernails across my desktop, fidgeted some more and shrugged.

This woman made coffee nervous.

"Thirty minutes."

"Start there, then."

So that's where she started.

Chapter Two

VALERIE MILLER'S HUSBAND, Paul, had been the creative director with Adkins and Associates Advertising, or Triple A as it was known in the biz, for eleven years. Advertising years are like dog years. Eleven years at Triple A equates to seventy-seven years in the real world. On a Thursday, three weeks earlier, Paul Miller had parked in the underground parking space allocated him six years earlier when he made creative director, and rode the elevator to his office on the fourteenth floor of Bow Valley Centre in downtown Calgary, where he set his briefcase down on the corner of his desk.

It was eight-fifteen in the morning.

By eight-thirty, he was out of a job.

The night before, Adkins and Associates Advertising had been taken over by Sumpter Advertising out of New York, Toronto, Los Angeles and Washington. It was not, in the words of Valerie Miller, a friendly takeover.

"The bastards screwed him to the wall," she said.

The suits from Sumpter offered Paul Miller six months

severance, three months full benefits, three months job coun-selling and a super buyout deal on his company Mustang.

Take it, they said.

Or leave it.

He took it and they shook his hand, averted their eyes, wiped their corporate brows and steered him gently but firmly out the door.

When he returned to his car, they had already removed his nameplate from the wall.

He did not go home immediately. He would tell me, later, that he drove aimlessly around the city for hours "in a total mindfuck," his brain shutting out the awful reality of what had just taken place. At forty-six, Paul Miller was under no illusions about finding another job tomorrow.

Or even the next day.

Eventually, he found himself out near the airport, watching the big planes roll in, and wondered what the hell he was going to do with the rest of his life. His wife, Val, had been a stay-at-home mom most of her married life, but their two children, Donna and Mitchell, now in their twen-ties, had left home years ago.

Val Miller liked to entertain on a fairly grand scale, especially since moving to an executive family home on the lake in Crystal Air, an upscale subdivision in Okotoks, a small but rapidly growing white-collar town just fifteen minutes southwest of Calgary.

Paul had leased the Lexus for her a year earlier. He was paying a six-figure mortgage on their lakeside home, plus rent on a house up in Varsity where his daughter, Donna, attended the University of Calgary. He owed for a big-screen

TV and a surround-sound home theatre system, carried two small life insurance policies and owed in the low five figures on a variety of credit cards.

He didn't tell me any of this. I found out on my own. It was the least I could do, since I was being asked to take him on as a client.

Against his will.

And without his knowledge.

Chapter Three

PAUL MILLER'S LIFE WENT even further down the proverbial toilet when he drove home around six that evening. In fact, it went around the bend, out the pipe and into the primordial swamp.

And that wasn't counting the interest accruing on his decision not to tell his wife he'd lost his job. He'd hoped to find a new one before telling her he'd lost the old one. He'd decided to take the counselling, send out résumés, line up some interviews and put a positive spin on life in general before 'fessing up. He knew his severance package wouldn't last long and it wouldn't get paid into his bank account for several more weeks, maybe a month. After calculating his running expenses, he decided to draw a chunk of cash from his current account right away.

He banked in Okotoks and stopped by the branch on his way home that night. He parked outside and entered the overly bright lobby. The lobby was partitioned off from the bank by floor-to-ceiling security gates.

When he arrived, both bank machines in the lobby were

in use. An elderly lady was making a cash withdrawal from one machine, and a scruffy married couple in their mid-twenties was crowding the other. When the elderly customer finished, she snapped her purse shut, clenched it tightly beneath her arm and scowled at him as she left.

Paul Miller slid his card into the machine and punched in his PIN. As he did so, the couple to his right began an intense whispered argument.

Miller glanced over at them.

The man jabbed a finger at the display screen.

"What's this shit?" he snarled at his wife.

Paul moved back a casual three feet until he could see the high-intensity backlit message of doom on the couple's bank machine.

INSUFFICIENT FUNDS

"Ah, fuck it!" the man hissed and hit the glass display screen hard with the flat of his hand.

The woman winced. She stood very still.

"Where's all the goddamn money?" the man asked her.

"It's spent," she whispered, a quiet tone Paul assumed was meant to calm the other man. "The car insurance. I told you they were gonna cancel it. And Paula's medicines. We can't go without, Vic."

"Fuck the insurance!" He smacked the screen again. "I told you they could wait!"

"Vic?"

She reached out, laid a hand on his arm, but he shook her off, the uncontained rage boiling up from deep within.

He turned to face her. She broke eye contact, stared hard at the floor.

"You can't keep driving without insurance," she said.

What was intended to reassure was interpreted as criticism.

Paul Miller saw the man boil over, a sudden eruption that had him swinging at his wife. She saw it coming and took a quick step back, trying to protect herself, but he caught her in the belly, doubling her over and driving her down to the lobby floor.

Appalled, Paul Miller grabbed the man by the scruff of the neck and threw him backwards across the open lobby.

And that was the view the security cameras caught.

Which was why Paul Miller was then charged with assault.

Chapter Four

WHICH DIDN'T SEEM FAIR.

"That doesn't seem fair," I said. "Losing his job and getting arrested, all on the same day."

As if an extra day might have evened up the odds.

"That's not all," Valerie sighed. "When Paul tried to help the woman up, Asshole rabbit punched him in the back of the neck, then kicked the living crap out of him."

"Ouch."

"Someone found him unconscious on the floor. He was bleeding from the head. It took fourteen stitches to close the wound."

"No witnesses?"

"None."

She fidgeted, needing a cigarette.

"So what do you need from me?" I asked her.

"Oh, it gets worse yet."

Paul Miller was a proud man. Having the crap kicked out of him by a man half his age was disconcerting. He stewed about it for days, lying in a hospital bed in High

River, twenty minutes south of Okotoks.

And then the Royal Canadian Mounted Police laid formal charges of assault against him.

"You could tell they were reluctant," Val said. "It was all Asshole's doing. He lawyered up and pressed charges, figured if he won, he could then sue for damages. Damages." She looked disgusted. "Right. He scuffed his boots on my husband's head." She looked away for a moment before continuing. "The cops felt that Paul would be acquitted, based on the severity of the attack against him. And they hinted it wasn't the first time Asshole had beaten the snot out of his wife."

"Is Asshole his first or his last name?"

"It's his middle name. Victor Asshole Shriver. His wife's name is Ruby."

"Let me guess," I said. "Ruby Shriver won't go up against her husband? She won't testify?"

She gave me a look.

"You know Ruby, do you?"

I didn't, but I've dealt with a lot of women in similar situations. Women who live every day in mortal fear of their husbands.

The wages of fear are paid with silence.

Val phoned Paul's boss early the next morning, to advise him that Paul wouldn't be in for a few days.

Quelle surprise.

Paul who? Paul Miller didn't work there anymore.

When she got over the shock, she went and sat at her husband's bedside for the next three days.

And never let on that she knew he'd lost his job.

He was discharged Sunday evening and spent the next four days pretending to go to work. He got up at the same time every day, showered, shaved, put on a suit, kissed Val on the cheek and drove into the city.

By Thursday, she'd had enough. That evening, she asked him why he hadn't been to the office in a week.

At first, he denied it, but when she told him she'd called his boss the previous Friday, he grudgingly admitted the truth. She understood his pain, empathized with his feelings of loss over a job he really enjoyed, a job that had kept the wolf from their door and allowed her to pursue a hedonistic lifestyle.

But what she couldn't understand was his decision not to confide in her. She felt betrayed, as if her support meant nothing to him.

In turn, he felt embarrassed. He felt ashamed that he'd lost his job. In keeping it from her, he'd hoped to spare her the humiliation that haunted him day and night.

A fierce argument ensued, and by the end of the night they were at each other's throats.

"And we've been there ever since," she said. She took a cigarette from the carton and twirled it a few times before shoving it away again. "Then on Monday of this week," she said, "my husband called his lawyer. He asked him to set up a meeting with Victor Asshole Shriver and Asshole's lawyer. They met yesterday." She turned and looked out the window for a while before continuing. "At which time my husband made Asshole an offer he couldn't refuse."

I waited.

"And it were a doozy."

She fidgeted some more but I waited her out.

"He offered to go three rounds in a boxing ring with Asshole if he'd drop the charges. Queensberry Rules."

She was right.

It was a doozy.

"Your husband," I said. "He's a boxer, is he?"

"No."

"A martial arts guy, then?"

"No."

"A street brawler, perhaps?"

She shook her head.

"A wrestler?" Head shake. "An ex-army commando?" No. "He has a cape and wears his underwear over his trousers?" A smile. Followed by another shake.

"He hit some kid on the nose when he was in grade three."

Finally.

Something to build on.

"What happened?"

"The kid's older sister pummelled him after school."

A sister?

Good grief.

"All right." I tried a different line of questioning. "What did Asshole say?"

"You need to understand how Paul set the thing up first."

Fidget.

"Sure."

"He called him a coward, undermined his manhood. Said he just got lucky at the bank. Said even though he,

Paul, was twice Shriver's age, he had bigger balls. He insulted him pretty good, made it virtually impossible for Shriver to say no and walk away with his manhood intact." She paused. "My husband's a risk taker."

"Clearly. You were there?"

She shook her head.

"I talked with Paul's lawyer."

"Shriver agreed? With his lawyer present?"

"The lawyers never stood a chance. There was way too much testosterone in the room for just two real estate lawyers."

"So, Shriver agreed?"

"Yeah. But not before he fired his lawyer," she said.

"And Paul?"

"He fired his lawyer too."

"This fight," I said. "What's its status?"

She looked at me and shrugged.

"Boxing," I explained, "is governed by a whole bunch of bodies. I don't remember them all but there's the World Boxing Association, the World Boxing Council and I think there's an International Boxing Organization. Those are professional bodies. Then there's the International Amateur Boxing Association. If they've agreed to fight, I assume they'll use a referee, and so I think they will have to be sanctioned. Hopefully, it will be sanctioned as an amateur bout."

"Hopefully?" she said.

"Yeah. Amateur boxers wear headgear."

"Like helmets?"

An image of two boxers wearing crash helmets formed in my mind. I shook my head.

"No. Think of the movies. When you see boxers sparring, they usually wear leather headgear."

"Oh. Okay. And that's good?"

"It's better than nothing. Headgear helps to protect against cuts and scrapes from the gloves. But it doesn't do anything to protect against a concussion."

"Why not?"

"Because it doesn't cover the chin. You get hit on the chin, your head snaps back. When your head stops, the bits inside keep going. Then the head snaps forward again and they slam against here." I touched my forehead. "That's how you get a concussion."

"Why do they call it the sweet science?"

"It's usually only managers and promoters who call it that."

She nodded, thoughtful for a moment.

"Have they set a date?"

She nodded.

"July thirteenth. A Friday," she said and pulled a face. "That's just eight weeks away." She stared at me. "I want you to stop it."

"Is that all? I thought you were going to ask me to do something difficult."

"Are you being a smartass?"

"I was going for derision."

"Well, you missed."

"My apologies. I will try again. Are you out of your gourd?"

"Probably."

"I'm a private detective. I detect things. I follow people

without their knowledge. I snoop in their garbage. I dig up dirt on them. How am I supposed to stop two consenting adults from punching each other's lights out? Especially when I'm in favour of the old guy."

She glared at me.

"My mistake. The more mature gentleman."

She took a long, deep breath.

"Look." She fidgeted some more. "I'm at my wits' end. This asshole is going to beat my husband senseless. He's half his age, strong as an ox and he's a street brawler. There's a very good chance he could inflict permanent damage on my husband. As in brain damage. God almighty, he might even kill him. I don't know what else to do, who else to call. You were referred to me. You're supposed to be a good guy. A knight in shining armour. And right now, God knows, I need a knight in shining armour."

I looked at her a long moment before answering. Clearly, she was distressed. And in her situation, who are you gonna call? Referrals are always nice to get. They mean somebody out there thinks you did a good job. They think enough about you to send you more business.

So how could I turn her down without offending the person who referred her to me?

I began to buckle.

It didn't take much. My funds were getting a little low. And besides, I really don't like guys who slap women around. So I guess I already knew I was going to take the job. I just I didn't know how to go about it.

Which was pretty much par for what I do. Annoy the hell out of people until somebody takes a swing at me.

And I go forward from there.

Assuming they miss.

"I'm not cheap," I told her.

"Neither am I," she countered.

"I'll give you a week," I offered. "Two grand plus expenses."

She inhaled sharply but she didn't argue.

She opened her purse.

"Cheque's okay?"

"We knights prefer alfalfa."

She looked blank.

"For our steeds."

More silence.

She might live in Okotoks but I could tell she wasn't a country gal.

"Our trusty horses," I said. "They eat alfalfa."

Ah.

She got it.

I didn't say she thought it was funny.

"I guess, in a pinch, I could take a cheque."

She filled it in and handed it across the table. I put it in my desk drawer without looking at it.

It seemed the white knightly thing to do.

She gave me a photograph of her husband, their home address and phone number printed neatly on the back.

Then she gave me the bad news.

"You can't let him know you're doing this, of course. Working to stop the fight." She paused. "I'm not sure what he'd do if he found out. In fact, I don't think you should even meet him."

I sighed.

I should have charged her double.

We shook hands and she rummaged for a cigarette before she was out the door.

"By the way," I said, holding her a moment. "Who recommended me?"

She leaned into the flame from her lighter, took a long, satisfying draw and blew smoke all the way to the ceiling before she answered.

"Yellow Pages."

After she left, I got my feet back on the desk, parked my hands across my ripply six-pack and stared at the ceiling. I had a feeling I might need help on this one but I was reluctant to call on Danny Many-Guns, my erstwhile business partner, spiritual adviser, mentor and best friend. Danny, a full-blooded North American Indian, shared my deep disapproval of wife beaters, but I was loath to stir up painful memories for him.

And me.

I stared at the ceiling even harder, looking for inspiration. It took almost a full ten minutes before I finally dozed off.

The phone awoke me a few minutes later.

It was Valerie Miller.

"I just remembered," she said, "it's called Workouts."

"What is?"

"The gym."

"What gym?"

"Where the fight's being held." She paused a moment. "Were you asleep?"

"No. I was being deeply inspired," I said.

"Right."

"Where is whatsits?"

"Workouts. It's over near the library."

"That would be the library in . . ."

"Okotoks." She was getting exasperated.

"Of course."

"Any leads yet?"

Leads? Good Lord, the woman was relentless.

"I thought I had one," I said, "but it went up in smoke."

She hung up. She might have slammed her cellphone down on me but it's so hard to tell with cellphones. There's no satisfying clunk that accompanies the slam anymore.

And they call that progress.

Chapter Five

I DECIDED TO RIDE MY moti-sickle to Okotoks. It was warm for May, and I'd had the battery on trickle charge for almost a week. And I was itching to take the bike for a blast. Danny had given me a couple of very profitable stock tips last year and I'd splurged part of my windfall on a new bike, trading my silver Honda Blackbird for a red one. It's a 1998 V&M anniversary 1200 SuperBlackbird. It's one of only fifty ever made, which only means something to me and the other forty-nine people who own one.

She fired up the moment I hit the starter button. My leathers were hanging in the small closet at the back of my office. I also wore my faithful, if slightly smelly, Alpinestar riding boots and a full-face helmet. Riding a bike is dangerous. Coming off at any speed can hurt like hell. I want all the protection I can get. Besides, I'm madly in love with an ER nurse named Cindy Palmer, who regales me regularly with horror stories of motorcycle crash victims crazy enough to wear less than I do. So I wear the leathers, in part, because, in her words, "it's less painful than having

20

someone like me change your dressings three times a day."

The other reason I wear leathers is down to the IRA. Yes, the Irish Republican Army. I'll explain later but you won't like it. MacLeod Trail was busy as usual, and I filtered east, over to the Deerfoot Trail. Most of Calgary's major routes are called trails for some long-forgotten reason. There's Blackfoot Trail, Sarcee, Shaganappi, Crowchild and a whole bunch more I don't remember.

People who ride motorbikes tend to stay off the Deerfoot. Six lanes of speed-crazy traffic, tailgating, switching lanes without warning, yakking on cell phones and doing God only knows what else. But the 'Bird has the speed to stay ahead of anything out there, so I ride it often. Once I'd crossed the Bow River and got down past McKenzie Town, the traffic thinned and I began to enjoy the ride. The sky was an endless blue, not a cloud up there anywhere, and the sun warmed my face through the dark visor of my helmet.

God was in His heaven and all was right with the world.

Well, the Deerfoot, anyway.

As I rode under the Marquis of Lorne Trail bridge, which is also Highway 22x, I spotted a pair of sport bikes coming down the on-ramp, accelerating hard like a pair of Phantom jets. I tracked them out of the corner of my eye. I was in the outside lane, holding steady around a hundred and forty klicks, about eighty-five, ninety miles an hour.

Fast enough in that traffic.

It didn't take them long to catch me.

I glanced over as they drew level in the centre lane.

Squids.

That's biker talk for teenagers on fast sport bikes. It isn't really meant as a put-down. And it's a pretty universal term. It simply means a youngster on a powerful bike whose skill set doesn't match the bike's performance. Which is probably true of most of us.

They both rode Gixers, which is Suzuki slang for some of their models. One was a six hundred, the other was the much more powerful one thousand. That's cubic centimetres.

Very fast bikes, both of them, but especially the one thousand. A real handful if you don't have much experience.

Or even if you do.

They were riding in denim jeans and jackets, running shoes and no gloves.

Which brings me back to the IRA.

During "the troubles," when the IRA was openly at war with the Brits in Northern Ireland, the IRA perfected a form of retribution for people they considered unfriendly to their cause. It was termed "kneecapping" and they shot offenders in the kneecap.

Or kneecaps, if they'd really pissed them off.

Since Ireland is a fairly small place, someone in the kneecapping crew often knew the person being kneecapped. If they put in a good word, the victim was then allowed to drop his trousers before being shot. This could make a considerable difference, especially if they were wearing denim.

As the bullet enters, it pushes millions of tiny denim fibres into the bloodstream. Blue-dyed denim fibres. These dyed fibres can cause major blood poisoning. According to some sources, there've been more deaths from blood poisoning than from the actual kneecapping.

So I wear leathers. Coming off a bike at high speed in denim can have the same effect as being shot in the knees. It's bad enough dealing with the aftermath of a spill. Who needs blood poisoning as well?

The squids looked over at me, giving me the universal "wanna go?" nod, but I just gave them a friendly wave back and let them go.

They crouched down, elbows high, kicked the shifter down two points and ripped the throttle wide open. They yowled away, accelerating up the box with prolonged, ear-piercing shrieks as they swept past the two-hundred-and-fifty-kilometres-an-hour mark.

That's a hundred and fifty miles an hour on a public highway.

I do believe they lock you up for that.

Assuming they can catch you.

The rest of my ride was fairly peaceful. Near its southern end, the Deerfoot crosses a wide, picturesque valley as it curves towards the old Highway 2, merging to form a four-lane stretch of blacktop heading south all the way to the U.S. border.

I peeled off right at the Okotoks exit where the road runs along a broad plateau, giving up views of the Rocky Mountains that tourist brochures refer to as "breathtaking, spectacular and awe-inspiring," usually in the same sentence. There was still snow on the mountains, and it shone a deep, rich white along a horizon that stretched for a hundred miles.

Awe-inspiring was right.

Maybe even spectacular and certainly breathtaking.

I couldn't look at that view without feeling a tug, without wanting to turn the bike west and head for the snow-covered hills and lose myself up in the canyons.

But that don't pay the rent.

A few minutes later, I cruised into Okotoks, the fastest-growing town in Alberta, maybe even Canada. The town sits along the Sheep River, which roars down from the Rockies every spring. It gets its name from an old Cree word meaning "stony crossing." Which is why you should wear your shoes when crossing the river.

Or use the bridge.

The big-box stores have settled the land south of the river, bringing a new prosperity to the town. Wal-Mart and Canadian Tire were the first to arrive, though I doubt they got their feet wet crossing the Sheep. Not everyone would agree that prosperity is a particularly good thing, though. I'm sure many of the older inhabitants wish their town was still no bigger than a button.

Elizabeth Street, the main drag, was busy, but I got lucky and found a parking spot at the east end, just past the traffic lights right outside the bank. I parked alongside a fire hydrant. I wasn't worried. I figured if the bank caught fire, I'd be the first to know.

I took off my helmet, roughed up my helmet hair, peeled off my gloves, stuffed them inside the helmet and carried it into the bank. The receptionist smiled as I approached the front counter.

"What a beautiful day for a ride," she said.

"It is indeed," I said, smiling right back at her. I'll smile at anyone who acknowledges the fact that I ride a bike.

"Who are you here to see?"

"Mr. Greyson."

She leaned forward and peered through the glass window of his corner office.

"He's got somebody in with him right now. Would you like to wait or maybe come back later?"

Ah. Small-town Alberta. You'd never get service like that in Calgary.

"I guess I'll wait."

"Have a seat," she said and waved me to a row of chairs across from her desk. "Can I get your name?"

"Eddie Dancer."

She scribbled a note on a slip of pink paper.

"I could hang up your jacket if you're finding it a little warm."

"I'm fine," I assured her, "but thank you."

Her phone rang then and she turned her attention elsewhere.

I sat for maybe ten minutes before the bank manager's door swung open and a young couple stepped out. Greyson looked to be in his early forties, five or six years older than me. And about forty pounds heavier. The result, no doubt, of a nine-to-five desk job.

He shook hands with the young couple, took the slip of pink paper from the receptionist, glanced at it and waved me into his office all in one fluid movement.

"Dwayne Greyson," he said.

"Eddie Dancer. Good to meet you, Mr. Greyson."

We shook hands and he took in my leathers.

"It's Dwayne," he said, and I nodded my assent.

He pointed me to one of two chairs in front of his desk as he sat down with a resounding plunk and all the air in his seat cushions escaped with a squeal.

He leant back in his chair and opened the venetian blinds six inches.

"Nice bike. What is it?"

I told him.

"Really? Pretty rare then. I'm more a Harley guy myself. My wife, bless her, prefers four wheels and a cup holder."

"You could get a new wife."

"Been there, done that. Which is why I can't afford another Harley."

We grinned, two guys sharing a life's-a-bitch moment.

We talked Harleys for a while. He loved the Soft Tail and I admitted to preferring faster bikes but I still could enjoy cruisin', too. A bike's a bike. As long as you've got two wheels under you, it shouldn't really matter what the tank badge says.

"Although," he said, "you never lose money on a Harley."

Everyone says that, so I guess it must be true.

"Maybe I should buy a Harley and keep it as an investment."

"You could do a lot worse," he said. Then he switched smoothly from Mr. Harley to Mr. Bank Manager. "So. How can I help you, Edward?"

I cringed.

Only my mother ever called me Edward. And since both my parents were dead, it always acted as a reminder of what was missing in my life when somebody used my full name.

I sat forward, elbows on knees.

"It's Eddie," I said. "And maybe we can help each other."

He acquired a sudden shrewdness. "Maybe."

He sat back and watched me. I wasn't buying his good-old-boy routine. He was friendly enough, but under the surface, Dwayne Greyson was nobody's fool. He was an astute judge of character and as shrewd as they come. I laid my business card on his desk. He glanced down but didn't pick it up.

"Private detective, eh?"

I nodded.

"Is this —" he paused a moment "— bank business?"

"Sort of," I said. He nodded carefully. "And what is it you need from me?"

"A few weeks back, a man got himself hospitalized in the lobby."

"Did he now?" He was no longer smiling.

"An elderly lady, a customer of yours, may have witnessed the altercation."

He said nothing.

"When this goes to court . . ." I paused and switched gears. "*If* this goes to court, some smart-assed lawyer might consider it iniquitous on the part of the bank if they were to withhold the lady's identity."

He looked at me for a long moment.

"Iniquitous?" he said.

I nodded, knowing full well he knew exactly what the word meant.

"Who are you representing, Mr. Dancer?"

Well, at least he wasn't calling me Edward anymore.

"The Miller family."

"And in what capacity?"

"I'm so glad you asked that. This is off the record?"

"Just between us girls," he said.

"You're aware that Paul Miller has been charged with assault?"

"That's common knowledge."

"Well, he made a deal with Victor Shriver a few days ago."

He waited for me to continue. I was pretty sure he didn't know about the fight.

Yet.

But Okotoks is a small town, and news travels at the speed of a phone line. I didn't feel I was breaking a trust by telling him. And I was fairly certain he would keep it to himself.

"He challenged Mr. Shriver to a boxing match. A real one. Three rounds in a ring."

Despite himself, Dwayne Greyson laughed out loud.

"You're kidding me?" he said.

"No. If Paul Miller wins, Shriver's agreed to drop the assault charges."

"Paul must have a death wish."

"You've met them both, I take it?"

"Haven't you?"

"I haven't met either of them."

"You just told me you're representing Paul Miller."

"I am. But I've been hired to stop the fight. Someone's worried Paul Miller might get hurt."

"They've every right," he said, speaking softly, as though not wishing to cast aspersions on Victor Shriver.

"So I'm trying to find out if the elderly lady who was here withdrawing cash from her account that night might have seen something I can use to persuade the RCMP to revisit the charges."

"Don't you think she would have contacted the police herself if she'd seen anything? It was the talk of the town for a whole week."

"Maybe. But maybe she doesn't realize how important she might be. Or that she could be in line for the reward."

"What reward?"

"The one I'm about to offer her."

He thought about it, he really did. But in the end, he had to go with being a good corporate employee.

"I'm sorry," he said. "I'd like to help but it's bank policy. You understand, yes?"

"Sure."

He made no move to end our meeting.

"So," he said. "Who is it believes we're being unfair?"

We were back to being iniquitous.

"Well," I said. "If the Millers' lawyer can persuade a judge that withholding her name is hurting his client's case, then he might get himself a subpoena. With the bank's name front and centre."

"And mine underneath."

"That distinct possibility exists."

"I like Paul Miller," Dwayne Greyson said. "We worked on the same committee at Rotary last year."

"And I'm trying hard to save his neck," I said. "I'm not looking to hurt him, Dwayne."

He gave me a look he hadn't learned on any Rotary

committee.

"That's good to know. Because if you did —" he picked up my card "— I'd know where to find you."

A veiled threat.

I was really beginning to like Dwayne Greyson. Maybe I should transfer my banking out to Okotoks.

I watched as he turned over the pink paper with my name on it, then printed the lady's name on the back.

Thelma Laurin.

He passed the slip of paper across the desk to me.

"I guess I can justify it, if it keeps the bank's name out of the papers. God knows, it wasn't the sort of publicity we enjoyed, having one client beat another client half to death in the damned lobby." He paused. "This is strictly off the record?"

"Everything we talked about is off the record."

"Good."

We stood up.

"I appreciate your help, Dwayne. And tell your wife I hear the new Harley Soft Tail comes with a cup holder this year."

His face brightened.

"Really?"

"Wouldn't surprise me if it did."

He grinned.

"Keep the shiny side up," he said.

Which was pretty damn good, coming from a Harley guy. We shook hands all over again.

"Go, Rotary," I said.

Chapter Six

THERE'S A REAL ESTATE OFFICE at the top end of Elizabeth Street, next to the PetroCan station. I pulled in around the back, double-checked that the kickstand was down and walked around to the reception area to borrow a phone book and a street map.

The duty realtor went out of her way to help me, even though I told her right off the bat I wasn't looking to buy a house today.

"Maybe tomorrow," she said with a smile, and offered me the closing room and a cup of coffee.

I thanked her but turned down the coffee.

There were two Laurins listed in the Okotoks phone book. The first one lived on Woodbend Way.

I punched nine and got an outside line.

The Laurin on Woodbend Way turned out to be a Larry Laurin, a loquacious retiree, bereft of teeth from the sound of it, whose wife had left him eleven years ago and whose mother, whom he hadn't seen in more than twenty years, still lived in her home town of Glasgow and wrote to him twice a month.

And I'd only asked him if he knew a Thelma Laurin. Which, of course, he didn't. I made a silent promise that if I ever got that lonely, I'd shoot myself or get a cat.

I thanked him for his life story and hung up. The other Laurin lived on Elma Street. Number ninety-four. I decided against calling and asked the lady realtor for directions. Elma Street ran parallel to Elizabeth Street, so I had only to ride around the block.

Elma Street is a picturesque treed avenue of quaint, older homes, many already a hundred years old or more. Half of them had been converted into retail businesses. Nothing big or garishly bright. No takeout chicken nugget restaurants here, just a nice mix of photographic studios, art galleries and high-class Italian gift stores. It was nice to see someone in the Okotoks planning department had some vision.

Number ninety-four was a tiny yellow bungalow, a private residence located between a two-storey bed and breakfast and a turn-of-the-century art-deco design studio.

The gate to Thelma Laurin's bungalow was latched shut and I made sure to latch it closed behind me. I'd locked my helmet to the grab rail on my bike and unzipped my jacket to look a little less threatening.

The walkway was overgrown, and the house sat behind an untended hedge. The front door was painted a brilliant bright yellow.

I rang the doorbell, which set a dog barking somewhere inside. After a clattering of deadbolts, the front door opened a crack. An elderly lady peered out with a wrinkled face full of suspicion.

"Mrs. Laurin?" I put on my best smile.

"What do you want?" she barked at me, competing with the dog growling from around the door frame.

Correction.

Dogette.

The little runt weighed less than an anorexic dormouse.

"Has anyone contacted you about the reward?" I asked her.

The door opened a few more inches. The dormouse came onto the step, yapping up a storm.

"The what?" She looked down. "Shut up, Tiny!"

Tiny did as he was told, sniffing at the cuff of my leathers. Or he may have been wiping his nose on the hem.

And he stood on tiptoe to do it.

"There might be a small reward for information about the altercation at the bank last month."

"Alter what?"

"The fight," I said. "In the bank lobby." I paused. "You were there, weren't you?"

"Maybe."

"Because if you were, you might be in line for a cash reward."

"Who are you?" Direct, still in my face.

I passed her my business card. She held it at arm's length, squinting, her lips moving slowly as she read every word.

"How much?"

"A modest sum. But it's cash. Entirely up to you if you wish to declare it." She glared at me some more. "Personally, I wouldn't."

She looked at me cagily before opening the door a little wider. She stuck her head out, looked both ways, then grabbed my arm and tugged me inside. Tiny began barking again but she quickly silenced him and slammed the front door shut behind me.

"How much is modest?"

"Depends what you saw."

She had shrewd blue eyes buried in a sea of overlapping folds. I wondered what, if anything, she'd told the cops.

"Who'd you work for?"

"That's private. And confidential," I said. "Meaning I can't tell you."

"Then git the heck outta my house."

"All right. Give me a penny."

"A what?"

"A penny. Then you've hired me and anything you tell me is strictly between us. It'd be against the law for me to repeat anything you tell me."

Well.

Against *my* law.

"How do I know you're really a private detective?"

I pulled out my wallet and let her compare my business card with my driver's licence, the name on my MasterCard, my American Express card, my Visa card and my health-care card. When she was somewhat satisfied that I was who I said I was, she handed it all back to me but kept the business card.

I was just happy to get my American Express card back.

"Wait there," she said.

She shuffled out of the front room and disappeared

down a darkened hallway. Tiny stood guard in case I decided to follow.

Or to boost the family silver.

The front room was cramped with overloaded furniture. Why do old folks hoard their belongings? I vowed never to do that.

If I ever grew that old.

The room had that peculiar old-folk smell. A little camphor, some A535 rub and a tinge of mothballs.

What's that old mothball joke? If you've got a mothball in this hand and a mothball in that hand, what have you got?

A bloody big moth.

I looked around the room some more. Every surface was crammed with trinkets, dusty little mementoes and reminders of her life. Small bunches of dried flowers hung from a plate rail that ran around the room. The flowers looked fragile and long dead, as if a good stiff breeze would blow them all away.

On the credenza against the far wall sat a photograph in a large, ornate silver frame. It was of a woman in her midtwenties. She wore the red serge of the RCMP, which clashed with her shock of red hair. Her face glowed with an open smile that crinkled the corners of her emerald green eyes. The Mountie had signed the photo, "Gran. With love, Nicole," but the ink was beginning to fade. Other, smaller family photos cluttered the top of the credenza but none had the stature nor the importance ascribed to the picture of her granddaughter.

Mrs. Laurin came back, short of breath. She handed me

a shiny new penny. I made a point of testing it between my teeth, hoping to make her smile, but her scowl merely deepened.

"All right," I said. "You're now my client. I'm working for you."

"What about the reward?"

"Tell me what you saw first."

She thought about it before waving me into a chair. I chose the armchair nearest the door. Clouds of dust erupted as I sank down into it. I tried not to cough up a lung. Mrs. Laurin lowered herself into the overstuffed chesterfield that took up most of the other half of the room and pulled her cotton print dress over her varicose veins.

Small mercies.

"All right," she said. "Whadda ya wanna know?"

"Tell me everything you saw that night in the bank lobby," I told her.

She ran her tongue around her teeth, as if to lubricate the works before plunging ahead. I leaned forward, not wanting to miss a word.

"I was cashing a cheque, taking a little money out. This couple came in, stinking up the place."

"How so?"

"He was smoking. I tol' him he couldn't smoke in the bank. He told me to . . . he swore at me. Damn trailer trash."

"Was she smoking, too?"

"No. Little mouse, she was. Never said a word. Hardly even looked up."

"What happened next?"

"I got my money. Someone else came in. That Miller

fella, I guess. He used the same machine as me."

"Then you left?"

"Yeah. Well, I left the bank. I was trying to cross the road but nobody'd stop to lemme across."

"You had the green light?"

"Pah! Who's got time to wait for the green light? Jeez. I don't even buy green bananas anymore." She paused and adjusted her dress downwards. "When I turned around and stepped back up on the sidewalk, he punched his wife in the breadbasket."

"You can actually *see* him do that?"

She looked into her lap. And then she nodded.

Which was odd.

Because sitting in that position, looking at her lap, she wasn't actually *seeing* anything.

I was pretty sure she was *feeling* it.

That's because we store everything as a memory. And we can only recall a memory three ways. We can either see it, hear it or feel it. It all depends how we filed it away.

When we are still very young, we display a preference for the way we interact with the world. Some people see the world: "I *see* what you mean, Eddie." Others prefer the audio version: "I *hear* you, brother." And then there are those who relate everything to their feelings: "I *feel* like the world is crushing me."

Even though we have a preference, we can still move from one state to another.

When you ask someone to recall something visually, as I'd asked Thelma Laurin to do, they will do two things. First, they will break eye contact. Second, they'll look up.

"What colour was your first bicycle?"

Ask anyone that question and they will look away, then they'll look up.

It never fails.

If you ask them to recall the words of a song, they'll look sideways. Ask them how they felt when they heard the song, they'll look down. It's what we all do in order to access those three memory states.

So when I asked Thelma Laurin if she saw something, she looked down and felt it instead.

She accessed a feeling. An emotion.

· Which was suggestive.

Of what, I wasn't sure. But I had a pretty good idea.

"I saw him hit her," she said quietly, almost under her breath. "Then that Miller fella reached over an' grabbed him. He threw him back against the glass. Jeez, I thought he was gonna break it. Miller went an' helped the girl. She was on the floor. An' he got hit on the back of the head for his trouble. Then Shriver started kicking him when he was down. Kicking and kicking and kicking. He was losing a lot of blood. It was horrible to watch."

She went quiet.

"Did he see you?"

A nod.

"Victor Shriver saw you watching?"

She bit her lip. Nodded again.

"Then what did you do?"

She wouldn't look at me.

"Nothin'."

It came out quiet, a small, shaky voice full of age.

"You left?"

She nodded.

"You didn't call the police?"

She shook her head. A tiny movement.

"But they questioned you?"

She looked at me then. Her eyes had lost the hard edge. She looked old and vulnerable.

"They had the bank video, the bank records. They knew I'd been there when it happened. I tol' them I hadn't seen anything. I said I'd left before anything musta happened."

"Why not tell them?"

She shrugged, but I could see she was frightened.

"Were you worried that Victor Shriver might come looking for you?"

A little nod.

"What else?"

She looked at me, a quick, appraising glance.

"Nothing else," she said, speaking quickly. She sat motionless for long seconds before she spoke again. "I was wrong," she said.

"Maybe," I said quietly. "Maybe not."

"Who are you workin' for? Besides me?"

"The good guys."

She struggled to get up off the chesterfield.

"I don't want no reward," she said, waving me off. "You just make sure he gits his."

Too late.

I'd already folded five fifty-dollar bills and tucked them under one of the doilies on the end table next to my chair. I'd take it out of my pay. I couldn't see Valerie Miller sitting still for an unreceipted two hundred and fifty bucks.

"I appreciate your help, Mrs. Laurin."

"It's Miss. I went back to my maiden name after my husband dropped dead."

Not passed away.

Not passed on or passed over or met his Maker.

He dropped dead.

And there was an edge to her voice when she said that.

She'd outlived the bastard.

You really didn't need to be much of a detective to figure it out.

I shook hands with her. Her skin was dry and loose over the little bones in the back of her hand and it was pitted with liver spots.

"You've done the right thing." I kept hold of her hand. "So you don't have to worry about Victor Shriver. Everything you told me is strictly confidential."

"Thank you."

"And your husband," I said. "He can't hit you anymore, Thelma."

Her chin began to quake.

"No." She lifted her head. It took an effort. "It still hurts, though."

I let her rest her head against my chest for as long as it took to get her composure back. I coaxed a smile from her as she closed the front door, then walked down the pathway to the gate. I latched it shut behind me and pretended not to notice the RCMP cruiser parked so close to my bike, its front bumper was resting against my back tire.

Chapter Seven

I WORKED THE HELMET over my ears and snapped the visor down. I looked at the lone occupant, sitting stiffly behind the wheel. Even with her hat pulled down tight, there was no mistaking the red hair or the piercing green eyes.

It was Thelma Laurin's granddaughter, Nicole.

She remained where she was, watching me straddle the bike. I fired up the motor and dropped it into first. For one long, irrational moment, I considered patching out, laying down a strip of burning rubber in my wake, just to piss her off.

But decided against it.

The price of back tires, and all.

Workouts was located in a brand-new two-storey building just east of the library. The parking lot was around back and I was surprised to find it was half full. It was mid-afternoon.

I parked under a canopy of trees, wrestled my helmet off my ears and carried it with me as I walked around to the double front doors. Before I got inside, the RCMP car rolled by, the lone lady occupant giving me the evil eye.

The air inside the gym was cool and slightly damp, and I heard the unmistakable thump of a bass that promised vigorous exercise in progress. I felt out of place, sheathed in leather.

The front counter was unmanned.

Unwomanned?

I pinged the chrome bell sitting squarely in the middle of the glass countertop and listened as it echoed off the walls and up the staircase to my right.

Nobody popped up with an afternoon smile.

I wandered past the desk, through another set of double doors into a room full of sweaty ladies. The music was almost deafening, a Pilates class in full swing. The women watched me in the floor-to-ceiling mirror but nobody stopped, nobody came over or offered me a place on the floor beside them.

I backed out, my head full of buttocks, many worth a second or even a third look, but I'm a gentleman and we don't gawk.

Which is why God gave some of us photographic memories.

I took the stairs two at a time to the upper floor, invigorated, no doubt, by the frenzied activity below.

Upstairs consisted of a weight room packed with Nautilus machines, free weights, treadmills, rowing machines and some other machines I had never seen before. A few people, mainly men, worked the machines, and a couple worked together with the free weights under the instruction of a guy in lime-green tights and a darker green T-shirt with the arms ripped out, the better to show off his biceps.

And triceps, since he had plenty of both.

He saw me watching and indicated he'd be with me momentarily. I waved him off and moved left towards the back of the gym where a full-size boxing ring was set up. The ropes were deep red against blue corner posts and the white canvas floor of the ring was edged with heavy yellow stitching. It was like no boxing ring I'd ever seen. It was way too nice.

Against the far wall, taking up maybe half the width, were the speed bags, three of them, and three heavy bags. Nobody was using them. An elderly black man was wiping down the last of them, spraying leather conditioner onto the bag and then working it into the dark leather in deep, lazy circles.

"Hi," I said, and he stopped what he was doing and regarded me with a certain amusement. I guess I looked out of place. "How you doing?" I said.

He nodded. He was doing just fine. Then he sprayed some more conditioner on the bag and worked it into the leather. I walked over to him, poked the bag with a finger. It barely moved.

"You thinking of joining?" he asked.

"No," I said. "But I was thinking I might hire you to work on my leathers when you're finished buffing the heavy bags."

He might have smiled at that but it was hard to tell. I got the impression he didn't smile much.

I studied him a moment. His face was cut in a million

tiny scars, the nose broken twice, maybe three times, the tissue around his eyes and mouth puckered and tougher than the leather he was polishing. I glanced at his hands. Big knuckles, gnarled now but they still carried the power of an oak tree. If he decided to use them.

"Were you pro?" I asked.

He nodded slightly. He didn't want to go there and that was okay.

I looked around the gym.

"This place." I shook my head. "A little too cute for me."

He moved his head up and down, maybe a quarter inch.

"You do much training?"

He misunderstood my question.

"Don't think they'd let me train you, you don't join their gym."

"Not me."

"Really? Don't need it, huh?"

He said it mockingly, showing me the chip on his shoulder. I guess he'd won his fair share of fights. But I guess he'd lost a few on split decisions, too. He nudged the bag.

"Show me what you got," he said.

Sometimes it's not easy being a guy. We walk into places and set ourselves up by the simple fact that we wear underpants rather than a bra.

I could have declined, of course.

And if you wear a bra, that's exactly what you'd expect me to do.

But if you wear underpants, you'd know there was no way I could decline and still pee standing up.

So.

"You want to hold it for me?" I asked him.

"You think you might move it?"

I unzipped my jacket, hung it over the top of the ring, and shook out my arms and shoulders, loosening up. He moved slowly, leaned lazily into the back of the bag.

I stepped forward.

I should have worn gloves, should have warmed up first, should have taken a few jabs to get the bag moving, to get some blood flow into the muscles, but I figured he'd tense up and I'd lose the element of surprise. So I walked up to the bag and let rip a punishing left hook, coming up on my toes as it connected, twisting from the hips, my stomach muscles ripped tight as I drove all my weight up through my shoulder and followed through, hard to my right, feeling the bag jump like it had suddenly received a strong electric shock and didn't like it one bit. I kept the momentum going and the impact rocked him backwards, forcing him to take a step back.

The heavy bag danced like a man on the gallows and I resisted the urge to smack it again. Instead, I reached out and held it, settled it right down, then stepped around it and looked at him.

"Maybe I *should* join. Whatcha think?"

"The fuck you learn to punch like that?"

"Kindergarten."

"Tough school," he said. "Y'ever thought of turning pro?"

I shook my head. "Tough way to earn a buck."

He nodded, looked past my shoulder.

"Good meeting you," he said.

He turned and got back to polishing the bag. I looked behind me, saw the Jolly Green Giant in his lime-green tights heading our way.

"Who's this?" I asked quietly.

"Boss Hog," he said under his breath.

Boss Hog walked on the balls of his feet. The lime-green tights were obscenely tight and the darker green T-shirt didn't quite cover his lunch. He was having two plums and a frankfurter today. Except the steroids that had pumped his six-foot-three-inch frame to almost three hundred pounds of heavy muscle had reduced his plums to raisins and his frankfurter to the size of a triple-A battery.

Or double A if he was really excited. He'd have looked better if he'd weighed ninety pounds and fronted a boy band.

"Can I help you?" Boss Hog asked, his rising voice tinged with impatience.

"Maybe you can."

He stopped in front of me. He was carrying a clipboard, bouncing up and down on his toes. Up close, I could see he was well past his prime. His close-cropped hair was dyed silver blonde, and he had deep lines around his eyes and forehead that even regular shots of Botox had failed to erase.

And he was wearing way too much aftershave.

His eyes were rattlesnake blue.

And he never blinked.

"You're looking to join, looking for a membership?"

"No." I smiled without warmth. "I'm looking for information."

He stared at me for long seconds, giving nothing away.

"What sort of information?"

"On the fight."

"The fight?"

We could go on like this all day. I'd say in July and he'd say July? Then I'd say Victor Shriver and he'd say Shriver? So I said, "Are you going to repeat everything I say?" and he almost said, "Everything you say?" but caught himself.

"Leave your name and number at the front desk," he said. "They'll let you know when the tickets go on sale."

Tickets? On sale? Oh, Christ. The plot just thickened. I looked at the area outside the ring and did a quick bit of math. I figured they could easily seat three, maybe four hundred spectators.

Not a bad night.

"How much are the tickets?"

"Haven't decided."

"Roughly?"

He shrugged.

"Fifty. A hundred, ringside."

He stood to make maybe twenty-five grand if he sold all the tickets. Which was very bad news for Valerie Miller.

"There's nobody on the front desk," I told him.

He handed me the clipboard.

"Leave me your name and number."

I took out a business card. Wow. Two in one day. Things were looking up. I slid my card under the clip, handed the board back to him. He couldn't resist a peek. His brow would have wrinkled but for the Botox. He gave me a last head-to-toe before dismissing me.

He turned to the black man polishing the body bag. "The men's washroom needs your attention, Adam."

The ex-boxer never said a word. He gathered up the leather polish and walked away. I stood next to the Jolly Green Giant as we watched him go.

I turned and looked at him with his silly spiked dyed hair and his girly aftershave. In a goddamn gym, no less. Who wears aftershave to a gym, for the love of Christ?

I shook my head.

"Scary, that is," I said.

"What is?"

"That he could pulverize one of us with his one hand tied behind his back."

I walked away.

Let him figure out which one.

~

The Pilates class was over when I reached the lobby. The reception desk was still empty but the instructor was nearby. I asked her directions to the washroom.

"The men's?"

I guess you don't need to be too bright to teach a Pilates class.

"That would be my first choice," I told her.

She pointed me in the right direction.

Adam was standing beside a wall of mirrors in the empty bathroom, rubbing away an imaginary blemish. I went to the row of urinals, picked the middle one and relinquished a cup of breakfast coffee.

"Are you training Shriver?" I asked him over my shoulder.

"Ha!"

"That a yes?"

"Punk-ass kid. Thinks he knows it all already. What's he want with a trainer, anyway?"

"So you're not?"

"So I am. So what's it to you?"

"He's fighting a man twice his age," I said. I jiggled up and down before zipping up. "A man who's never had a fight in his life. Desk job. Company expense account, three-martini lunches, expects to go three rounds with this kid."

I washed my hands.

"You looking to make a buck?" he asked.

I stuck them under the hand dryer.

"You think there's a chance?"

"If you bet on the old guy," he said.

"Really?"

"To lose."

Chapter Eight

I CALLED VALERIE MILLER on my cell phone from the parking lot of Workouts a few minutes later.

She was home.

"Hi," I said. "Do you know who this is?"

"What?"

"I'm being circumspect. In case your husband's home."

There was a pause.

"Oh. It's you. No. He's not home."

"So you're okay to talk for a minute?"

"What do you need?"

I was actually phoning to bring her up to speed about the gym selling tickets, but there was something she might be able to help me with.

"Do you know an RCMP officer in town, name of Nicole?"

"Yes. Nicole Laurin. She's the one who came to see Paul in hospital. She felt real bad about giving us the news. About the assault charges," she added. In case I'd forgotten about them. "Why do you ask?"

"Nothing specific," I told her. "But I do have news for you. And not good news."

"Jesus. An' I'm outta cigarettes. They say bad things happen in threes."

"They are planning on selling seats to the fight."

"Who is?"

"The gym."

"Well, if you do what you're hired to do, they can't, can they?"

"The point is, if your husband's agreed, if he's signed a contract, it could get rather expensive to back out."

There was silence on the line. Then, "How expensive is expensive?"

"Depends on the ticket price. At fifty bucks a pop and a hundred for ringside, they'll scoop around twenty-five grand. Plus souvenirs, popcorn, Coke sales, say another six or seven grand. So maybe thirty-two, thirty-three thousand dollars. They'll be looking for compensation."

There was a longer silence.

Then, "Oh, shit."

"So. What are your instructions?"

No hesitation this time.

"Stop the goddamn fight."

She hung up.

Holy crap. Maybe *she* should fight Victor Shriver.

I know where I'd put my money.

Chapter Nine

I KEPT MY SPEED ten klicks over the limit as I left town and hit the four-lane highway but that wasn't good enough for Officer Laurin. She lit me up from behind with the party-light bar and hit the siren a couple of sharp yips, pulling me over a mile out of town. Even though at least four cars and five trucks blew past me before we stopped, all way above the posted limit. I parked up and took off my helmet, resting on the tank while she took her sweet time.

"In a bit of a hurry there, sir?" she asked.

I pointed to the high-speed offenders zipping past in the outside lane.

"What, you couldn't catch *them* guys?"

"I'm not concerned with *them*, guys. Sir."

"But *them's* all going faster than *I* is. Was."

"It's their lucky day then, isn't it? Sir."

I looked at her and decided I didn't like her very much. She had aged, marginally, since she'd signed her name on the photograph in Grandma's house, but aging had improved her looks. And don't let anyone tell you a tight uniform doesn't flatter the female form.

This one did.

And then some.

I let her see me look over my shoulder so she knew that I knew she'd been alone in the car when she stopped me. Then I gave her my licence, registration and pink slip.

"Just so you know, I have the time to fight a ticket." I smiled. "And the inclination."

Fighting a speeding ticket in court would tie her up for at least half a day. And since she was alone, it would be her word against mine. But on the downside, if I were the judge, I'd take her word over anybody's, any day of the week. Still, I have a clean licence. That's not to say I don't get tickets, I most surely do. But I spent two years as a Calgary city cop and I maintain good contacts in the police department. I have to, to do my job. So I don't have any speeding tickets registered to my licence. Which might help if the judge were sympathetic to me. And if I could call into question Officer Laurin's calibration accuracy.

"You did calibrate your speedometer today, didn't you, Officer Laurin?"

She looked surprised that I knew her name.

She took my paperwork and thumbed through it. The fact that she didn't take it back to the cruiser told me she'd already run my plate.

"Why are you harassing my grandmother?" she asked.

"I'm not harassing anyone's grandmother," I said.

"Why'd you go and see her?"

"What did she tell you?"

"I'm asking you."

"Client confidentiality. Breach of trust for me to tell you anything."

"You telling me she hired you?"

"Somebody hired me."

"You really expect me to believe that?" she asked.

"Why don't you ask Granny?"

I folded my arms across my chest, enjoying the sound the leather made as I did so. Meanwhile, another dozen vehicles blew past, well above the speed limit.

"I intend to," she said.

And I realized, of course, she'd already asked her. And Granny had gone Velcro-lips. Well, what do you expect? She told the cops she hadn't seen anything at the bank. She was hardly going to go back on her word now, was she?

"Nicole. I'm not here to hurt your grandma. I'm working on the side of the angels."

"Sure you are."

But before she could pursue it any further, her radio crackled a code that had her running to the cruiser. She tossed my papers onto my tank and took off, slamming the cruiser into drive. She spun the wheel hard left and gunned the motor, spitting loose gravel from beneath the back tires as she patched out onto the highway.

Then the highway traffic suddenly found Jesus and slowed to the posted limit.

I watched her party lights disappear and put my papers away, tucked a few stray locks under my helmet, got back on the highway and pinned the throttle to the stops. I figured, since the police presence was in front of me, who was going to nick me for being over the limit this time?

A few miles ahead, the four-lane highway from Okotoks joins Highway 2 north to Calgary. It crosses the bridge over Highway 2 before peeling off into one of the greatest high-speed, two-lane corners in the province.

Well, not a legal high-speed corner but then who's counting?

Looking down from above, the road curves beautifully from twelve o'clock all the way around to nine o'clock in a perfect radius, two hundred and seventy glorious degrees that disappear under the bridge before they slingshot you northbound to the Calgary city limits. On a bike, you can take either lane at in excess of seventy miles an hour.

If you know what you're doing.

And if you are wearing knee sliders to protect your knees from scraping the tarmac.

Officer Nicole Laurin had pulled her cruiser off to the left, beneath the bridge.

It was one of the squids.

It was pretty obvious what had happened. They'd come around the bend tight together on the outside lane. The kid on the bigger bike, the one-thousand cc machine, putting out nearly one-hundred-and-seventy horses to the rear wheel, had seen the road opening up ahead of him and had whacked the throttle wide open. Which would have been okay if he were on the six-hundred cc machine with maybe a hundred horses to the back wheel. But on the bigger, far more powerful one-litre bike, he'd totally over-throttled it. Where throttle balance between life and death is measured in millimetres, he'd gone for big yardage.

And paid the price.

His back tire had broken loose, leaving a deep black rubber scar down the outside lane.

Which had probably terrified him.

So he had throttled back, which is the most natural thing to do when your back wheel breaks loose around sixty, maybe seventy miles an hour. It's also the worst thing you can do at any speed. When he'd cut the revs, the back wheel had slowed down and the tire had found its grip, snatching the bike upright. The whiplash effect had thrown the rider clean over the handlebars.

It's called a high-sider.

He'd landed on the road, probably bounced a few times, and then the blacktop had torn his jacket and jeans to shreds. It was after the skin on his back. He'd come to a stop just shy of the northbound lane. It was pure luck that he hadn't been run over. I parked up close to Laurin's cruiser, pulled off my helmet and ran to help. I crouched across from her. She had her back to the oncoming traffic.

The kid was still conscious. From the angle of his left leg, it was obviously broken in several places. His left shoulder didn't look good, either. Miraculously, he'd been wearing a back protector under his jacket. It was the only thing that had stopped him from being skinned alive.

His helmet had a deep crack, front to back.

"Can you hear me?"

He was already in shock, his eyes open wide, looking terrified. He'd bitten his tongue, and blood flowed from his open mouth. I didn't know if he understood me. I glanced up at Officer Laurin. Which probably saved her life.

An eighteen-wheeler pulling not one but two big trailers

was heading north. The driver was trying to pull to the left, trying to get into the outside, overtaking lane, but his trailer was swaying violently, almost out of control. As he roared past, the trailer came back across the inside lane. It was headed straight for Nicole Laurin.

With no time to warn her, I reached across the boy, grabbed a handful of Nicole's jacket and yanked her out of the path of the trailer as hard as I could. She came crashing down on top of me. We ended in a pile of limbs and I heard her cry out, more in surprise than in pain.

I hoped.

The passing trailer clipped her ankle.

It was more like a passing swat that did no real damage other than make her mad.

"Goddamn it!" She untangled herself and stood, yelling up the northbound highway, shaking her fist at the rapidly receding tail end of the rig that had nearly claimed her life.

The boy, miraculously, was untouched. I heard the wail of an ambulance way off in the distance. Nicole Laurin turned to face me.

"Holy crap," she said.

She looked pale.

"You okay?" I asked.

She took stock of herself.

"Yeah."

I turned back to the boy lying on the road. He was staring up at me, looking scared and confused.

"You came off your bike," I said. "You've bitten your tongue. An ambulance is coming. Are you feeling any pain?"

His mouth moved. I leaned closer.

"No."

"That's a good sign. Don't try and move, though. I think you've broken your leg."

"What happened?"

"You don't remember?"

He tried to shake his head, thought better of it.

"No. I felt the bike start to slide." Sudden panic now. "What happened to the bike?"

I looked over. It was pretty beat up, fifty yards down the road.

"Needs a paint job."

"Oh, shit. My brother's gonna kill me." He tried to sit up but Nicole put her hand on his chest and he lay back.

"Where's Barry?"

"That your buddy?"

A small nod, followed by a wince.

"He's directing traffic."

I was being nice. He was doubled over, throwing up.

Nicole took a turn interrogating the kid.

"What's your name?"

"Dave. Dave Hunter."

She started making notes.

We heard the ambulance coming closer.

"Whose bike were you riding, David?"

"My brother's. He's in Afghanistan. He's in the army."

The ambulance wound its way down from the overpass.

"Does he know you borrowed his bike?"

The ambulance doors flew open. The paramedics jumped out, hauling out a stretcher. The wheels dropped like an undercarriage.

"No," he said. "Man. He's gonna kill me."

The paramedics arrived at the same time as the pain. His face contorted, his mouth opened wide, and he let out a real scream.

"Good timing," I told the paramedics.

I moved away, over to where Barry was coughing up the last of his lunch. Okay, the last of his breakfast, too. He saw me coming, tried not to look guilty.

"Is he gonna be okay?"

"Sure. He'll be fine. Until his brother finds out." I steered him away as the paramedics prepared to lift Dave on the stretcher. "So, tell me what happened."

It was pretty much as I thought. They'd been howling around the bend, neck and neck. When they hit the apex, they had both opened up the throttles.

"Dave's bike suddenly went crazy. It threw him straight over the bars. How we both never came off . . ." He shook his head at the near miss. "I saw him hit the ground. Then I almost ran into the bridge. I couldn't stop fast enough."

He looked like he was going to throw up again.

"Did you talk with him?"

He looked guilty. He just shook his head.

"It's okay. You're in shock, too."

"He's my buddy. I couldn't go to him. I was so scared of what I'd find. I thought he was dead."

"He's not going to die."

They had him on the stretcher and were carrying him to the ambulance. The traffic had slowed in all directions, everyone rubbernecking as they cruised by.

Nicole Laurin was walking alongside the stretcher, holding up a plastic bottle of clear liquid. I hope he liked morphine.

Above us, a pair of fire trucks wound their way down the ramp, coming to clean up the mess. "What speed were you doing?"

"We were fast," he admitted. "Real fast."

"You might want to keep that to yourselves," I said. "It wasn't speed that did him in. It was losing traction. His back tire spun up. The Gixer puts out a lot of power to the back wheel."

He looked at me closely, took in the leathers and the riding boots, and then searched around for my bike. He recognized it immediately.

"Ah, shit. Are we in trouble?"

"Not from me. But promise me you'll stick to the posted limits after this."

"Christ. I'm not sure I'll ever ride again."

"Well, that's up to you. But if you do, get yourself some proper gear. And the two of you take a course."

Nicole came over then. She smiled nicely at Barry, putting him at ease. She introduced herself and asked him if he was up to sitting with her in the cruiser, answering a few question.

"I guess."

He probably thought I'd still be there when they were finished. I retrieved my helmet, fired up my bike and filtered into the northbound lane. I had no wish to stick around any longer than necessary. I'd done precious little for Dave, just kept him talking to offset the encroaching effects of shock. He was in much better hands now. I passed the ambulance as it crested the hill. They were taking him to Calgary. I wondered if they were taking him to Rocky View.

Probably.

With any sort of luck, he'd draw the long straw and Cindy Palmer would feed him ice chips and change his dressing three times a day.

Wow.

That almost makes it worth falling off your bike.

Chapter Ten

IT WAS WELL PAST MIDNIGHT when I noticed my cell phone flashing. I was watching the Stones on DVD, and I paused the concert, took off the headphones and checked the message on my cell.

It was a voice mail from Nicole Laurin, asking me to call her. I dialed her up on my land line, and she answered on the second ring.

"I never got chance to thank you properly," she said.

"No need."

"Yes, there is. You saved my life. My husband wants to thank you, also. In fact, we want to recommend you for a commendation."

"No." I sat up straight, horrified at the thought. "Nicole," I said. "I appreciate the gesture but I can only do my job if I'm out of the spotlight. It might help save *my* life one day if I stay below the radar."

"I see." She sounded disappointed. "But we need to do something. You really did save my life out there."

"And if I'd been on the outside and you'd been in my

shoes, you'd have done exactly the same thing."

She thought about that for a moment.

"Maybe," she said. "But not with the same speed. I've never seen anyone react that fast."

"Pure luck. I'm glad I could help. How's David doing? Any news?"

"Last I heard, he'd broken his leg in three places. Plus he's lost a lot of skin off his thigh. They weren't expecting him out of the OR for a couple more hours. I guess his leg's a mess."

"Will he be charged?"

"He already learned far more than we could teach him."

"Good for you."

"I understand you're helping the Miller family."

"Maybe."

"In which case, you'll appreciate knowing what you're up against."

"Have you been checking up on me?" I asked.

"You have a good rep with some Calgary cops. I'm sorry for busting your balls. If there's anything I can help you with —" she paused "— off the record?"

When my ship comes in, I'm usually at the airport. Time to make proverbial hay.

"What can you tell me about Victor Shriver. And his wife?" I asked her.

"Well, Victor's got a couple of D.U.I.s. We've tried to hang an assault charge on him a couple of times but Ruby won't press charges. She's a sad case. Been with him since she was fourteen. Had a baby a few years back. I think Ruby's maybe twenty-seven, twenty-eight now. No record, she keeps to herself, and she's skinny as a rail."

"Is she a stay-at-home mom?"

"Yeah. I see her around town sometimes. The baby's always sick; she brings it into the clinic."

"Same old same old."

"Yeah. I guess this is nothing new to you, either."

"I wish. Anyway, I really appreciate the help," I said.

"Do you have a fax?"

"I have two. One at home and one at the office."

"Where are you now?"

"I'm at home."

"Give me that one."

So I did.

"You didn't get this from me."

"Get what from you?"

We hung up and I went back to my DVD. I was watching the *Licks* world tour — three concerts on three DVDs. The ones in the black and green box. I've watched the Rolling Stones in concert hundreds of times.

And I never grow tired of them.

Unlike real life.

Chapter Eleven

I LEFT HOME VERY EARLY the following morning, well before sun-up. And yes, I rode the motorbike. Never a moment's hesitation. People die every day. They die crossing the street, brushing their teeth, flushing the toilet. Some even die jumping out of airplanes. So, with the possible exception of the latter, I had no intention of stopping doing any of the above, either. Before I left, I phoned the Rocky View. After being bounced around a few times, I said I was David's brother. They told me he was still under sedation but that his surgery had gone okay. Which I took to mean he still had two legs.

I rode downtown to my office in Victoria Park. I needed the Jimmy so I parked the Honda in its reinforced, padlocked shed at the rear of the office. I fired up the Jimmy and patched out of the parking lot without bothering to check in at the office. I knew once I got up there, I'd never get away. I hadn't done the *Herald*'s crossword puzzle yet.

I headed south down MacLeod and thought about the job in hand. Since Boss Hog was planning to make a bunch of money selling fight tickets, my chances of stopping the fight had diminished considerably and, since the client still insisted I stop the damn fight, that's what I was planning to do.

There was the possibility that neither Victor Shriver nor Paul Miller would actually want the fight stopped. Valerie Miller's insistence that I not make contact with her husband was okay for now, but if I needed to talk to him in order to succeed, then contact him I must. Short of burning down Workouts, I couldn't see any other way to stop the fight right now.

My main concern was this: Suppose Victor Shriver was quite good? Suppose he had the ability to really mess up Paul Miller? To put him, this time, well beyond the reach of the hospital staff and all their facilities? Valerie Miller was right to be concerned, and Paul Miller was a fool to think he could go three rounds with a street brawler, Queensberry Rules notwithstanding. Men have died after a single blow to the head in the boxing ring. In fact, according to Wikipedia, my online source for almost everything, more than three hundred and fifty people have died in the ring in the past sixty years.

But it's the tens of thousands who've suffered irreparable brain damage who've really paid the price. Which is one of the reasons boxing is banned in lots of countries. And some of them surprised me.

Such as Cuba.

And North Korea.

Makes you think, eh?

But not to worry, I had a plan.

Well, sort of a plan.

As plans go, it was actually the dumbest plan I'd had in a long, long time, but it still qualified as one.

The plan was, I would engage Victor Shriver in the manly art of fisticuffs myself. If this Shriver/Miller fight did materialize, I needed to know what Paul Miller was up against. According to my research, there are only three types of boxer. There's the in-fighter, the out-fighter and the brawler, and between them, they only use four different punches.

The in-fighter is the most exciting to watch because he likes to work in close, to get under his opponent's guard, to stand toe-to-toe and slug it out. He rarely uses more than two punches: the hook and the uppercut. And either one can kill you.

The out-fighter prefers to stay outside his opponent's reach, stepping close only to inflict moderate damage from his arsenal of two other punches: the jab and the cross. The out-fighter rarely knocks his opponent out, winning, usually, on points.

The brawler, still considered the low man in boxing circles, usually relies on brute strength and a single punch — a hook or an uppercut — to knock his opponent out.

The other reason I decided to pick a fight with Victor Shriver was to find out if he could take a punch. Many would-be boxers can put together a good combination, a good one-two punch, but they can't take the same sort of punishment. They have what's called a "glass chin."

Officer Laurin's fax to me the night before was a real time-saver. She sent me Shriver's home address with a hand-drawn map. Shriver lived on eighty acres east of Highway 2 and, without the map, I'd probably never have found it. She included a mug shot and, while it lost a lot of definition over the fax, it was good enough that I could pick him out in a crowd. At the bottom, she'd added a footnote that Shiver hung out at Steve's Bar and Grill in Calgary's northeast. It's a biker bar off Seventeenth Avenue and while I don't know it well, I knew how to find it.

It was just past seven by the time I located the Shriver acreage. I was curious to see where they lived, maybe see how they lived. The more I knew about my opponent, the better the odds I could defeat him. The entrance to their acreage was overgrown and the driveway was nothing but compacted brown mud. According to the Range and Township map, the property was close to the county line. It was a relatively flat piece that sloped to the east.

I parked the Jimmy on a gravel pad a hundred yards south of their entrance and jumped the drainage ditch, scrambling up onto the Shrivers' land from the southeast corner. I had my digital camera tucked against my ribs, under my jacket. I moved cautiously at a low crouch. The land ahead rose ten feet, and I dropped to my belly, elbowing my way to the top of the rise.

The house lay a hundred yards directly ahead of me, to the east. It was a trailer. What realtors call a mobile home.

A bijou residence.

It looked to me the kind of place that you kept your shoes on and wiped your feet when you left, although there was a pair of worn cowboy boots sagging against each other on the front porch. The porch roof also sagged but so did the porch itself, so I guess it all evened out. Plastic sheeting covered the front windows, and a rain barrel stood off to the right. It had overflowed, leaving a long, reddish-brown stain on the earth.

An old Ford Granada, more rust than original paint, was parked in the yard. A dog lay close by, a length of chain holding him firm to a metal stake hammered into the brown earth. At least, I hoped like hell it held him firm. He was a big old brute. He lay on his side and looked to be asleep.

To the left of the trailer stood a solid-looking barn. I ducked below the brow of the rise and scampered fifty yards to my left before elbowing my way back to the top, along a narrow gully that snaked down from the top of the rise.

Through the gap between the trailer and the barn, I could see a second trailer, set back maybe a hundred feet from the first one. A washing line of pink baby clothes hung in the sun and a motorcycle leaned against the porch. Between the trailers rose a short red pipe, growing up through a circular wooden collar. I figured that would be the well. The septic systems had to be a certain distance from the wellhead, seventy feet if I remembered correctly. Which would put them out of sight on the far side of the trailers.

The dog lay to my right. He hadn't stirred. I risked a neck-stretching, prolonged look around the place. It was pretty shabby. Grass grew through the abandoned hulks of half a dozen rusted trucks and cars and both trailers shared the same shabby chic. They were set in a low depression, hidden from the prying eyes of neighbours, who were all a good half-mile away.

I put the camera on the grass in front of me and lay down and waited. For what, I wasn't sure. Lying in the narrow gully, I was well-concealed from all sides. If anyone came up the driveway, I was well-concealed from them too.

It was a nice place to fall asleep.

After about two hours, the door to the far trailer opened and a woman in a long, thin dress stepped outside. I got her in the camera lens and zoomed in close. She was rail-thin, in her late twenties, and I could see the last of a purplish bruise fading beneath her jawline.

Ruby.

She crossed to the washing line, feeling each piece of clothing before deciding whether to take it down or let it dry some more in the morning sun. I fired off a dozen close-up shots of her. My camera had been programmed to mimic the sound of a shutter. But it was too noisy for me, so I had disconnected the sound. Now it shoots in silence.

As I lay in the gully, focusing on Ruby, I realized what fine bone structure she had. Her blonde hair was limp and lifeless and she was without makeup.

And yet.

There was something quite beautiful about her, about the way she moved, the way she turned and held her face to the sun; the way she held her hair back and let the morning light caress her. A gentle wind stirred the thin fabric of her dress, pressing it against her, and I wasn't sure if she wore anything beneath it. Why would she? She had no idea she was being watched. Her hip bones stood out like a little pair of Derringers strapped in place.

I wondered if they were loaded.

As I watched her, I knew Victor Shriver did not deserve this fine and delicate creature.

70

Without warning, the dog raised his head and looked in my direction. I thought he was going to let it go at that, but he mustn't have liked what he saw, for he stood up and began barking. His shorthaired hackles were up and he strained hard against the chain. Every time he barked, both his front legs came off the ground. There was no mistaking the fact that he'd seen me. He lunged against the chain, trying to break free.

Ruby laid the dry clothes aside and hurried down the intervening space between the two trailers.

"Brutus!" She called to him quietly but sweetly. "Quiet, Brutus! Good boy!"

I fired off a few more shots before sinking quickly back into the gully. I could still see them through the concealing clumps of dried grass.

Brutus ignored her, barking and straining hard against his leash. I lay still and held the camera tightly, ready to take off if the dog chain broke, hoping like hell I could outrun Brutus.

And if I couldn't?

I'd climb a tree.

An ornithologist, photographing the Greater Warbling Gumshoe. Or was that the Lesser Warbling Gumshoe?

Who knew?

The front door of the first trailer suddenly flew open and a man in his mid-fifties came out, wearing jeans with the fly wide open and no shirt. His long hair fell over his face as he struggled to get both feet into the leaning boots on the porch. I pointed the camera at him and fired off a fast half-dozen shots, my fear of discovery in temporary abeyance. He straightened up and I could see ridges of muscle bunched in anger. There was little fat on him and he looked fiercely tough for a man his age.

Like a well-preserved stick of dynamite.

Ruby came around the corner of the older man's trailer and reached for the dog. She caught him by the collar and the dog stopped barking. He turned and licked at her, his stubby tail wagging a hundred miles an hour.

The man stepped down off the porch and went towards them.

"Shut the fuck up!"

It was clear by the way she jumped that Ruby hadn't seen him coming. The dog tried to twist away from Ruby, to hide behind the hem of her dress, but he wasn't quite fast enough.

The man kicked him across the hindquarters. The dog yelped loudly and ran in a half-circle, limping badly. The man followed him.

"I told you to quit that fuckin' noise!" He scooped and threw a handful of dirt and stones at the dog. "Now shuddup!"

"Roy! No!"

Ruby straightened up and faced the man. But she was clearly intimidated. The dog cowered, unable to escape the confines of the chain. I got my feet under me, ready to intervene. I wasn't going to let him kick the dog twice.

Not without extracting a similar punishment.

Ruby spoke from the heart.

"Please, Roy. Don't."

The man suddenly turned on her.

She met his eye for maybe a full second before dropping her head down, her eyes focused on the hard-packed ground. The man said something I couldn't catch, then turned towards his trailer. As he walked past the dog, he stomped his foot and Brutus scattered sideways, cowering again behind Ruby.

The man spat in the dirt at Ruby's feet and walked to his trailer. He didn't bother taking his boots off when he stormed inside.

Ruby knelt and patted Brutus, resting his massive head in her lap. He fell against her, shivering, and she kept stroking him and talking softly until he finally began to relax. She looked up at a sound, turned to face the barn.

A young man in his mid-twenties, wearing jeans and a T-shirt and sweating heavily, came out of Ruby's trailer. His arms were wrapped in dark tattoos. He wore his hair much longer than it was in the fax photo, tied back in a loose ponytail, but there was no mistaking him.

It was Victor Shriver.

The T-shirt clung tightly and he looked to be in good shape, with little or no body fat and very good muscle definition.

An inheritance from his father.

Along with the brutal temper, no doubt.

He shouted to Ruby, asked her what all the noise was about.

"Just Brutus," she called back.

"Well keep him quiet!" Victor said, and Ruby nodded. He bowed his head and lit a cigarette, snapped the lighter shut. "You going to town?" he asked her, blowing smoke into the warm morning all around him.

She nodded.

"I need the car."

"I'll be back by then."

He stood and stared at her, then turned and walked back into the trailer without another word.

So that was Victor Shriver.

He didn't look so tough to me.

Plus he smoked, so his wind wasn't as good as it could be.

I was beginning to look forward to having a go-round with this nasty piece of work.

Hey.

Everyone's job has a little upside.

Chapter Twelve

THE ROAD ON WHICH I'd parked ran straight south for another half-mile and then ended abruptly. I could see a deep cut of trees in the near distance and guessed the Sheep River flowed across the land to the south. I turned around, rode back past the entrance to the Shriver acreage and kept going up to the main road. I was pretty sure Ruby hadn't left yet. I would have seen her dust from the gravel, hanging like a rooster tail in the still morning air.

I parked a couple of hundred yards east of the T-junction, tucked in close to a metal gate that opened onto a field of cows. Judging by the grass wrapped around the lower bars, it wasn't a gate that had been used in years. I waited for almost an hour. I'm used to waiting, and while I'm still not very good at it, I am getting better. My mind used to wander and pretty soon I'd get bored and unfocused.

Then one day, Danny Many-Guns asked me, "What's the most important moment of your life?" and I recalled a major life-changing event from the past. I was wrong, of course. The most important moment of your life, he said, is this one. The here and now. To be alive at this moment means you have survived all the other moments that came before this one. This moment, then, is the most important. Which is why it is so important to live in the now, to remain in the present. He said it makes the waiting easier, too.

Living in the moment is a little harder when you are slowly roasting to death in a black leather pie-crust, visited by swarms of noisy and nosy flies, drawn, perhaps, by the overpowering smell of cow dung wafting in from the field next door. At that moment, I'd have paid good money to live in a different moment.

And did I mention the mosquitoes?

Sheesh.

A plume of grey dust announced Ruby's arrival, and not a moment too soon. I watched her slow at the junction before turning left, pulling away from me, heading towards Okotoks. She was driving the rusty Ford Granada and kept her speed below the posted limit all the way into town. I followed her at a distance. She turned into the parking lot at Extra Foods, the first supermarket in Okotoks, just down from the D'Arcy ranch golf course.

I waited for her to unload the baby and wrestle a shopping cart from the cart corral before I pulled in alongside her. The car was clearly on its last legs and I felt a pang of guilt, knowing what I was about to do. I gave her a one-minute head start and then followed her into the store. The vegetable section was off to the right and I took a few moments to select what I wanted: three of the largest potatoes I could find. I only needed one, but what kind of loser goes shopping for one potato?

I paid for them at the express checkout and walked back to the Jimmy. I waited until it was fairly quiet in the parking lot and made sure nobody saw me pretending to tie my shoelace behind the Granada; made sure nobody saw me pick the largest of the three potatoes from the bag and ram it firmly up the end of her exhaust pipe. I rotated a complete three-hundred-and-sixty degrees, then pulled it off, leaving a three-inch-long plug of raw potato firmly wedged inside the tailpipe, effectively sealing off the exhaust system, thereby preventing the car from starting.

As long as she didn't have a hole in the exhaust.

I dropped the rest of the potatoes into a nearby garbage can and went inside the store again. Ruby had finished her shopping and was laying her few meagre but essential items on the conveyor belt. I walked around the store until she was ready to leave, gave her a thirty-second head start and followed her out.

She was strapping the baby into the car seat when I got there. I hung back until she was behind the wheel before heading to the Jimmy. I could hear the whine of the Ford motor trying to start. It coughed, spluttered, died a few times before she pumped the gas and tried again.

Same thing. Lots of coughing and spluttering before the engine died.

I took my time getting into the Jimmy. I made eye contact with her and gave her a quizzical look but she looked away quickly and ground the starter motor again.

It was obvious, even to Ruby, that the battery wouldn't take much more of that. She sat with her hands on the wheel, frustrated. I powered down my passenger side window. She saw me from the corner of her eye and cranked her window down partway. She looked embarrassed.

"Would you like me to look under the hood?" I offered. "I've a set of jumper cables if that'll help."

She turned and looked over her shoulder at her baby in the child seat, then turned to face me. She took a deep breath.

"Do you have a phone I could borrow?" she asked me, shyly.

"Sure."

I stepped out, walked around, handed her my cell phone.

"Thank you." Her voice was barely above a whisper.

"Pop the hood," I said, smiling. "Can't hurt to take a look."

She reached under the dash and popped the hood for me. She kept the window down and I could hear her whispering into the phone: "Please, please, please answer."

I raised the hood and the flood of gas almost bowled me over. I fiddled with the HT leads, pretending I understood the nest of wires amid the oily grime beneath the hood, knowing nothing I did up front would make a lick of difference. I leaned around the upraised hood.

"Try it now," I said.

She cranked the motor and the battery lasted five more seconds before it ran down. I heard her smack the wheel and I closed the hood.

I walked up to the open window. She handed the phone back to me.

"Any help?"

She shook her head. I guess Victor was out in the barn by now.

"Would you like me to call a tow truck?" I said.

She shook her head, looking worried.

"Could you tell me what time it is?"

I checked my watch.

"Almost noon."

She sighed and looked up at me.

"Thanks."

I smiled at her, a warm, you-can-trust-me kind of smile. I noticed her eyes were the palest blue and her skin was almost translucent. I wondered what sort of life she'd had. But of course, I already knew.

"Sorry I couldn't be of more help," I said, resting my hand on the door a moment.

I started walking away, then turned to face her.

"How far do you have to go?"

"Long ways," she said.

"Look, if I can be of any help, I'd be happy to give you and your baby a ride home. And your groceries."

She kept her head down, shook it.

"Well, I have to shop for groceries myself, so if you change your mind, the offer still stands."

I left her to ponder her options while I went inside the store and did some grocery shopping, careful not to buy anything that would need to go in the fridge, since I had no way of knowing when I might get home. I was gone maybe ten minutes and she was still there when I came out.

I could hear her baby crying long before I reached the Jimmy. I unloaded my groceries into the Jimmy before I spoke to her again.

"Well, good luck to you," I said.

"Could I please borrow your phone one more time?"

"Sure."

I passed it through the window and moved away, watching as she dialed. I waited almost a minute before she hung up.

"I appreciate the offer and all, but I don't live in town."

"Me neither," I told her. "I'm heading into Calgary, but I've got time to drop you. As long as you don't live twenty miles in the other direction."

"We live east of the overpass. About ten, fifteen minutes."

"It's practically on my way," I said. "Listen, why don't we go inside. I'll give my business card to the store manager. He can take down my driver's licence number, too. I'm sure that would make you feel a little better about accepting a ride with a stranger."

She shook her head.

"And he can write down yours too," I said. "In case I'm offering a lift to some homicidal serial killer."

She almost smiled at that. And, silly as it was, it convinced her.

The store manager wrote my licence number on the back of my business card and put it in his shirt pocket. She promised to call him when she got home in one piece. We transferred the baby seat into the back of the Jimmy, she put her groceries next to the baby and then climbed in the front. I looked over my shoulder. The baby was looking around at the strange new surroundings. I couldn't tell if it was a boy or a girl.

But at least it had stopped crying.

"Are you a cop?" she asked as I backed up.

"A cop? No. Why would you think that?"

"Your business card," she said.

"I'm a private detective," I said. "But I used to be a city cop. Years ago." I drove across the parking lot, out to the traffic lights. "I'm working on a case here in town right now."

She didn't say anything. Maybe she was being polite. Or maybe I was boring her silly.

"I'm supposed to stop a fight. A boxing match."

She sat like a stone.

"Couple of guys are going to go three rounds in a boxing ring down at Workouts. The gym?"

She stared straight ahead as I made the left turn onto Highway 2. I began to wonder if Victor had even bothered to tell her what he was up to.

Then, finally, she spoke.

"Did you do something to my car?"

She was way too bright.

"Why would you think that?"

She turned and looked at me and I saw a spark moving deep within those pale blue eyes.

"Did you?"

"Yes."

She said nothing, just stared at me. A hard, glacial stare.

"Since we're being honest," I said, "let me ask you a question."

She didn't answer.

"Why do you stay with him?"

"What business is that of yours?"

"I have an aversion to guys who beat up women."

She said nothing.

"But that's not why I gave you a ride."

"Really?"

"No. It has to do with the reason I was hired."

She remained silent.

"The wife of the man who's getting into the ring with Victor is worried that Victor might do him serious harm."

I could barely hear her when she spoke.

"She should be."

"Which is why she's hired me to stop the fight before it starts."

"How do you plan on stopping it?"

"No idea. Not yet."

"What does all that have to do with breaking my car?"

"I wanted to talk to you."

"Hello might have worked."

"I doubt it."

"Men." She spat the word out like there was something nasty in her mouth. "You're all the same."

We rode in silence for a while and I licked my wounds. Finally, I spoke again.

"Is there any chance you'll help me?"

"No."

"Why not? Paul Miller stepped in and tried to help you while he was in the bank. He did the right thing by you. And spent almost a week in hospital for his trouble. Don't you feel you owe him something for that? Or are you just going to sit by and let Victor destroy him?"

She turned away and watched the countryside slide by the window. After two miles of total silence, she finally looked at me.

"You don't know my husband," she said. "You make him out to be such a bad person. But he's not."

"He beats you."

"Says who?"

"Are you saying he doesn't?"

"Why do you answer a question with another question?"

"Says Paul Miller."

And a witness who saw it all through the window.

"Are you saying he didn't hit you?"

"No." Her voice had dropped to a whisper.

"If you help me stop the fight, maybe I can help you too."

"I doubt that."

"Try me."

She shook her head.

"I have a lot of friends," I said. "People who can protect you, give you and the baby a safe place to live. I guarantee he'll never find you."

She looked me full in the eye for long seconds before I looked away.

"I don't need your help," she said. "I love my husband."

"You love that he beats you?"

"You don't understand."

"That's what they all say." And the moment I said it, I wished I could take it back.

Her eyes filled with tears but she fought hard and spilled not a drop.

"I'm sorry," I told her. "I had no right to say that."

"No. You didn't."

I signalled, braked carefully and made a right turn.

And realized only afterwards that I'd made a stupid mistake.

"How did you know where to turn?"

Because I'm an idiot.

She told me to stop at the entrance to their acreage. She climbed out and I tried to help her with the baby seat but she warned me off. She lifted the baby onto her hip and left the car seat, along with her groceries, just inside the driveway. I offered her my business card.

"I really don't like you," she said.

I tucked my card down between her and the baby.

Then she walked away, up the long drive.

"Don't forget to phone the store manager," I called after her.

I had visions of being arrested on charges of kidnapping.

This was becoming the sort of case I really didn't want.

Chapter Thirteen

I FELT SHITTY ALL THE WAY HOME. I swung by Extra Foods and dug the plug from the Granada's exhaust before Victor showed up with his toolbox.

When I got home to my little two-storey in Marde Loop, a fashionable part of Calgary, I showered off my sins and called Cindy Palmer, the true love of my life.

She caught the phone on the third ring.

"Don't," she said.

"Don't what?"

"Don't ask me out for supper," she said.

"Wasn't going to," I lied.

"I've been called back in to do an extra shift."

"Didn't you just work the day shift?"

"And when I got home, there was a message on my machine telling me I had to work the night shift."

"Is that even legal?"

"Can I hire you to beat some people up for me?"

"Gladly. No charge. In fact, I'll pay you."

"Good. Now tell me you weren't phoning to ask me out for supper."

"I wasn't."

"How disappointing."

I couldn't win, no matter what I told her.

"How long do they want you?"

"Until two."

"I'll pick you up then."

"No, Eddie. That's way too late."

"No matter. I'll take you home and massage your feet."

"Well. Lindsay's at her dad's."

Lindsay is her only child. Cindy and Lindsay's father divorced years ago. She's masterful, holding down a job and raising a fourteen-year-old daughter almost single-handedly. And just lately, her ex-husband began taking more of an interest in his daughter's welfare.

I think he feels threatened by my presence. Or he doesn't trust me being around his daughter. Who can tell?

"So maybe you'll get more than a foot massage," I offered.

"I love it when you talk dirty."

"But only if you wash your feet first."

"Pig."

"I have a tub of strawberry-vanilla-mocha body cream from Body Shop."

"I meant 'pig' in the nicest way," she corrected.

"And it's good with bagels."

"Idiot."

"Go save somebody's spleen."

"We're actually doing reconstructive rectal surgery."

"What the hell is that?"

"Do you really want to know?"

"No," I said. Then I thought about it. "Why would you

do that? It's not like the world is actually short of assholes."

"Damn it. I always give you the best lines. And what do I get?"

So I told her.

"Does that come with strawberry-vanilla-mocha body cream?" she asked.

I think she blushed at my answer.

I know I did.

And I almost forgot the other reason I phoned her.

"Can I impose?"

She didn't answer, by which I assumed I could.

"Ruby Shriver."

"Spell it."

I did.

"When do you need it?"

"When's good?"

"I'll bring it home with me."

"Did I tell you I loved you?"

"Loved?"

"Love," I corrected.

"Attaboy."

She hung up.

I forgot to ask her what she was wearing.

Chapter Fourteen

BY NINE, STEVE'S BAR WAS hopping. There were more beards bellied up to the bar than I'd ever seen in one place.

And that was just the women.

ZZ Top blasted down from industrial-sized speakers hung from the ceiling and the place was awash in cigarette smoke and beer fumes. This was one bar where the City of Calgary was going to have real problems trying to enforce the no-smoking bylaw. I tried to imagine a bylaw officer handing out no-smoking tickets. Over ninety percent of the biker dudes were smoking.

And by default, so were the other ten percent.

I'd parked my bike at an all-night gas bar a couple of hundred yards away, up on Seventeenth Avenue. Steve's wasn't the sort of place at which sport bike riders were made welcome. If it didn't say Harley on the tank, it didn't belong in the parking lot. I slipped the gas jockey ten bucks with the promise of another ten if he kept my pride and joy safe while I was gone. He offered to wax it and lick the carbon deposits off the tailpipe for the extra ten.

Just before I reached the bar, I took a bunch of five- and ten-dollar bills from my wallet and shoved them into the rear pocket of my jeans. I put my wallet back in my jacket.

You had a choice at Steve's. You could either order from the bar, manned by four heavyweight dudes with enough tattoos between them to put the Sistine Chapel to shame, or you could order from one of the waitresses, who all wore leather tank tops and miniskirts slightly wider than my trouser belt.

But not by much.

I ordered a beer from one of the barkeeps and took the bottle to the far corner of the long bar, my back tight against the wall. The door came in off a side street and the long bar was on the opposite wall. The four barkeeps kept the beer coming and looked perfectly capable of handling pretty much anything that came through the door. I settled in for what might be a long night, with no guarantee that Victor Shriver would even show, or that he hadn't already been and gone. I nursed my beer and watched the room. To my right were bistro tables. No stools, no chairs, just a few dozen circular tables, four and a half feet high. Each table was bolted to the heavy wooden decking that served as a floor.

To my left was the pool action. Six full-size pool tables, in three rows of two. Beyond the tables were two doors, hand-painted with BIKERS and BITCHES over the top, and a third door beneath an exit sign that opened onto a back alley and the loading area. The bar itself was maybe forty feet long. The wall behind the bar was covered in mirrored glass with shelves full of booze. The other walls were festooned with old bike parts. Carbs, magneto covers, kick starts, clutch plates, headlight rims, pistons and con rods. Given the time, you could probably build a couple of dozen bikes from all the spare parts nailed to the walls.

There were at least a hundred people in the place. Maybe seventy guys, the rest women.

You'll notice I didn't call them ladies.

The noise from the crowd rose and fell as people were pushed, pushed back, spilled beer on themselves, on each other and on the floor.

And some of them even managed to drink some.

The serious action was around the two pool tables closest to the exit. A lot of folding money changed hands on the outcome. Not on each game, but on each shot.

"Another?"

I turned. The barkeep had already popped the top off a second beer.

"Sure." I tossed him five bucks. "But you keep that one." I didn't need two beers tonight, thank you very much.

He scooped my five bucks, nodded a quick thanks and moved on to serve more serious drinkers.

Victor Asshole Shriver finally arrived around ten-thirty.

I watched him nodding to folks here and there. He made eye contact with another half a dozen guys before hitting the bar. The barkeep took his order without appearing to recognize him. Victor took his beer, turned to face the room, propped his elbows on the bar, leaned back and took a slow pull from the long-necked bottle.

Just like he belonged here.

And he was an easy fit. Beat-up leather jacket, worn and faded blue jeans, motorcycle boots, a red-and-blue bandana over his hair, his ponytail hanging ragged over his collar. I pretended not to notice him. Turned my attention elsewhere. All the pool tables were in use. At the table closest to me, two guys were playing for five bucks a game. I'd already noticed something a little odd about the taller of the two. Not that he was particularly tall, just that his partner was really short. The taller guy looked the part, a biker relaxing, playing pool. But there was something about the way he stood that made him stand out.

To me, anyway.

He was clearly a leftie from the way he played pool, yet he led with his right. By that I mean, he stood with his right hip forward. So he kept his left hip back. It was a cop stance. I know, I did it myself. When you're used to carrying a gun, you learn not to lead with your gun hip. If you do, you're just inviting some cowboy to make a play for it, to try and grab it from your holster. So you learn to keep that hip away from the action. It becomes second nature. Even when you're not carrying your gun, and he clearly wasn't, you still do it.

He was also nursing his beer. Pretty much the same as I was. He'd stand the bottle upright in his mouth, cover the opening with his tongue and swallow air. Then he'd bring the bottle down and give a good old boy belch. Letting all the air back out. When you use the washroom, you just fill the bottle up with water. Another undercover cop trick. Beats getting hammered every night.

When Victor Shriver pushed off the bar and sauntered over to the pool tables, he passed within three feet of me. We were almost the same height and weight, just built differently.

Where I was lean for my height, he carried his weight up high, in his shoulders and across his chest. And he was one of the few clean-shaven guys in the place.

I watched him dip his right hand into his pocket, then pull it out, as another guy sauntered past. Their hands touched. Quick and smooth. It was hard to be sure but the guy making the buy gave it away when he looked down to check out the goods. And I saw the tightly packed baggie-wrapped brown weed disappear into his pocket.

Ships that pass in the night.

And I wasn't the only one who'd noticed.

The undercover guy noticed it too. I could tell by the way he turned his head, the way he appeared so nonchalant, chalking his cue and turning back to make his shot. He wore a sleeveless denim jacket over a black T-shirt and leather pants with heavy-duty motorcycle boots. He was playing the role of a hangaround, a wannabe biker who hangs around with full-patch bikers, picking up crap work detail, hoping one day the club will patch him over, making him a full-fledged member. It's the only way you can become a member of most biker clubs. You start from the bottom. And there's no guarantee. You could be a hangaround all of your life, never climbing the lucrative ladder to biker heaven. All depends on who you know.

Or what you know.

I watched the crowd carefully, but I couldn't spot any other undercover cops. So maybe this one was off-duty, though that was unlikely. Even undercover cops have better things to do with their off-duty time than hang around biker bars.

I turned my attention back to Victor.

He scored at least three more drug deals in the next ten minutes. I wasn't sure how people knew he was holding. Maybe the signal was just showing up. In the old days, guys selling drugs had signals they were carrying that changed every week. Now, with cell phones and Blackberrys, signals were probably obsolete.

Victor stood with the betting crowd, watching the game at the table closest to the exit. He drained the last of his beer and it looked like he was getting ready to split.

It was time for me to go to work.

I switched my wallet from my jacket to the back pocket of my jeans, where I'd stuffed the loose five- and ten-dollar bills, and slid between the pool tables, moving up on Shriver slowly. When I got close, I affected a slight stagger, pretending to be more than a little drunk. Shriver was watching the game and holding his empty bottle in his right hand. He parked it on a shelf that ran around the end wall and hooked his right thumb through his belt loop.

I took the loose bills from my jeans, concealing them tightly in my hand. I moved in front of him, pretending to watch the game. After a few minutes, one of the players pushed by me. I moved to give him room and felt my ass bump Shiver's leg. There was nowhere for him to go; he was tight against the wall. I stayed put, my rear end resting against his right hip, and I dropped the handful of bills on the floor.

Shriver became uncomfortable, eased away from me. I felt the pressure slacken, took a quick step backwards and patted my jeans.

"Hey!" I spun around to face him, looked down. Twenty-five bucks of my money lay scattered on the floor. I pulled my wallet out. "You thieving bastard!" I yelled, enraged at having my pocket picked.

I shoved him in the chest.

The crowd parted.

"Fuck you!" He pushed me and suddenly everyone could see my money on the floor, my wallet in my hand.

"You picked my pocket, you scumbag!" I yelled at him and poked him hard in the chest.

He poked me again, just as hard.

"I never touched your fuckin' money! Get the fuck outta my face!"

I wasn't backing off.

He stepped forward, his hands held low, then snaked them out into my chest real fast. I let him move me several feet and wobbled to stay upright.

That's as far as we got inside the bar.

"Take it outside!"

It was the barkeep. The one who'd served me. He had a raised baseball bat in one hand, the other on my chest. And he didn't seem to care whose head he cracked open first.

Someone banged open the exit door and a stream of onlookers poured out ahead of us, cheering the evening's first scrap.

Someone else scooped up my money, shoved it into my hand. I pushed it into my pocket without taking my eyes off Shriver. As he walked towards the exit, past the wall rack, he snatched a pool cue, holding it tight to his body as he half-turned, waiting for me to catch up.

"Come on, fuckwad," he said.

When he saw that I was following him, he stepped outside.

The exit door opened onto the loading area, a forty-foot square of concrete surrounded by the high back walls of other buildings. Everyone spilled out with us, jostling to lay bets on the outcome.

Even the undercover cop put down a few bucks.

I wondered who he was rooting for.

Either way, I was happy to see him out there. He might step in and stop the fight if one of us looked like he was about to die.

Especially if it was me.

Chapter Fifteen

HE MADE NO PRETENSE ABOUT the pool cue. This wasn't a crowd that was hung up on rules. I was hardly out the door when Shriver came at me, chopping the pool cue double-handed from way up over his head like it was an axe splitting a log, the thick end coming straight down towards the top of my head.

I moved fast, more a lean than an actual step, and turned inward. The pool cue brushed past my forehead. I was already pulling my right shoulder back, and the thick cue whisked past me and crashed into the concrete. The impact stung Shriver's hands. Before he could recover, I stepped on the thick end, trapping the cue against the concrete beneath my boot. He was holding it in both hands, about level with his groin by this time. Before he could react, I walked up the cue, grabbing a random shoulder in the crowd for balance. It didn't take but a few seconds before he dropped it, unable to hold my weight with the sharp end of the cue digging into his palms. It made a loud crack as it hit the concrete and I flicked it away into the crowd, who cheered my circus act opening.

I squared off in front of him, forearms vertical, fists clenched, like an old-time pugilist. I did a little fancy foot-work and ended it with a fake stumble. I wanted to lure him into a fistfight, not a kickboxing event.

"Put up your dukes, old chap," I said, in a British accent that would have gotten me booed off the stage of *Pygmalion*.

The crowd appreciated it though, and gave a dull roar of approval.

Shriver backed up, scanning the crowd for the pool cue, but it was long gone. Now it was just him and me. He prob-ably carried a knife, as I'm sure most everyone frequenting Steve's place did, but I was figuring he wouldn't be stupid enough to use it.

He stood back and let me come to him. His defense was cocky and he kept his chin up, his arms hanging loose by his sides. His stance invited the quick jab that would snap his head back so a person could finish him with a left hook.

Or a right hook.

I didn't mind which.

I was an ambidextrous boxer.

I moved up on him and deliberately stepped on his lead foot, his left one, trapping him for a brief moment, just long enough to throw a short jab to his ribs.

He was quick. Despite the distraction of having me standing on his toes, he was focused enough to block the jab. Not that I put much into it. I figured I'd attack him at about half speed. He countered with a jab of his own, bouncing it high off my shoulder, and followed it with a quick right cross that brushed the whiskers of my goatee.

Hmm.

Not bad.

He was an out-fighter, preferring to stand back and pick his shots. I mirrored him. Whenever he threw a combination, I threw the same punches back at him, but with slightly less force and at only half my real speed. He ducked, bobbed, weaved and slipped left, but I still managed to land every punch. I watched his eyes and he telegraphed a lot of his punches, setting up his footwork an instant before throwing anything dangerous. I let many of his jabs connect but deflected his straight shots and his cross punches that were aimed at my head and face. He was in better shape than I'd expected and neither of us was scoring anything significant.

The crowd was getting restless.

Then he changed his game and almost caught me off guard. I'd hit him with a couple of jabs to the side of the head, then whacked him with a pulled straight shot to the chin. I expected it to sting, which it did, and it made him mad. But instead of backing off, he stepped inside my guard and switched to in-fighting.

The crowd loved it.

I could smell beer and cigarettes on his breath, he was that close, and he swung at me with a right hook that landed hard on my left shoulder. It stung, too. He followed with an uppercut but it was an obvious punch and I swayed, letting his clenched fist sail harmlessly upwards, missing my chin and my nose by half an inch. He stayed in close, though, and hit me with a flurry of right hooks to the upper body. He even got in a couple of Mexican hooks. They call them "rips" and for good reason. They're liver shots and they'd get him thrown out of the ring in a real hurry.

I fought back, switching to hooks and uppercuts myself. When you fight bare-knuckled, you need to be very careful you don't damage your hands. There are twenty-nine bones in the hand and all of them are breakable. There's a real science to punching, to keeping the strike zone of the knuckles in line with the wrist and the elbow. Get it wrong, just once, and you could break your hand or your wrist. He had many failings but by far his worst was his tendency to hyperextend his elbow. When he hit me with a jab or a cross, he locked his elbow. And I had to resist the temptation not to turn in and hammer a short, crippling blow to the back of his elbow joint. Such a blow would put him in a full arm cast for the next eight weeks.

We went toe-to-toe for almost a minute. His stamina wasn't bad, but he was breathing hard and it was all through his mouth. He was leaning against me and a couple of times he tried to knee me in the groin. The second time he tried it, I pushed off against him and hit him hard with a left and right hook to the head. I put a little more English on them and he backed up and looked at me shrewdly. I think he knew then that I hadn't been giving it my all.

And after that, he kept his knees out of my groin.

There was blood on both our faces. My lip was bleeding a little and he had a cut above his right eye that wouldn't stop bleeding. The blood ran all the way down his neck. But by now, I'd learned all I needed to know about Victor Shriver. I knew both his strengths and his weaknesses.

Unfortunately for Paul Miller, the former far outweighed the latter.

I decided to change a few gears of my own. I'd been fighting him like most boxers, leading with my right hand. Now I switched to fighting southpaw and led with my left. I moved towards him with my right foot in front, holding my left hand back to deliver the knockout punch. A few people in the crowd figured it right away and began changing their bets, switching the odds in my favour. Shriver didn't like it one bit. He tried to push me away as I advanced on him, but all that did was open him up down the front.

I hit him four good blows. Two quick jabs, enough to bring his head up and keep it there, then two fast left hooks. He stumbled backwards, spitting blood from a newly split bottom lip. I backed off and dropped my arms, feigning tiredness.

Enraged, he came at me, the brawler now, swinging an overhand right, holding his fist like a club, aiming to smash it down in my face. I sidestepped to his right and opened up the perfect shot, exposing his whole right-side jawline as he moved past me. I hit him with a hard straight shot to the jaw, snapped his head sideways, then uppercut him under the ribs. While he blew out what little air he had left, I swung around in front of him and hit him three more times in the stomach. Hard, flat smacks that punched every last inch of air from his body. He dropped to his knees, mouth open but nothing working, sucking hard to get the air inside, but it wouldn't go. There was no way he could get up. The crowd roared for me to finish him but he was already finished. I couldn't hit a man when he was on his knees.

Someone began a ten count. The crowd quickly picked it up and the swelling yell of numbers echoed around the walls. Shriver tried to regain his feet. Then he realized that if he did, I would hit him again. He sagged back on his heels and spat more blood on the loading dock.

"Nine . . . ten!"

The crowd booed and cheered in accordance with how much they had made or lost, and money changed hands at the speed of light. The crowd began to shove itself into the bar, eager to get to their beer.

There was no reason for me to go back inside. I pulled Shriver to his feet, stood him upright, made sure he wasn't going to keel over, and then walked away, cutting between the buildings to come out on the street alongside the bar.

I knew I had to find a way to keep Paul Miller away from Victor Shriver. If I didn't, I knew which one of them wasn't going to make it to the end of Round Three.

Christ.

I doubt he would make it to the end of Round One.

Chapter Sixteen

HALFWAY BACK TO THE GAS station to reclaim my bike, I heard the sound of somebody coming up behind me.

"Hold up!"

It was dark out there and I couldn't be sure who it was. Maybe Shriver had friends who wanted to even the score. I backed up against the building. No point letting anyone come up behind me. I grabbed a handful of loonies and toonies from my change pocket. First line of defense. If you're being swarmed by a gang, throw a handful of heavy coins as hard as you can at a few heads.

He stepped into the light.

It was the undercover guy.

And he was alone.

"That was quite a show," he said.

I shrugged like I didn't know what he meant.

He looked at me, strong and steady.

"You played him pretty good," he said.

"How so?" I asked.

"Acting drunk. You're no more pissed than I am. And

you could have nailed him at least a dozen times back there."

"I'm not *that* good."

"Never shit a shitter," he said. "You're better than he is." He stood on the sidewalk, watching me. "So. I'm curious. Why'd you set him up?"

"Why'd you want to know?"

"I'm just curious by nature."

"All right. But let me ask you a question first."

"Okay."

I dropped my voice to almost a whisper.

"Do you normally carry a gun?"

He looked wary, glanced around to make sure we were alone.

"Why would I do that?"

"Walk with me," I said. "My bike's up at the gas station on Seventeenth."

He kept a good six feet between us as we walked. He was having a hard time figuring me out.

"You haven't answered my question," I said.

He thought about it, decided against answering and asked me again why I'd set up Shriver.

"Do you know me?" I asked.

He looked over, shook his head.

"I used to be a cop."

"Bullshit to that."

"I didn't care for the discipline. So I quit and went private."

"You're a private eye?"

"Aye, aye." I held out my hand. "Eddie Dancer."

We shook hands and he tried to pretend my name meant nothing to him. Which it probably didn't, if he really wasn't an undercover cop.

"Gary," he said. "Gary Vaughan."

"I'll show you my ID," I said. "Then maybe you want to grab a coffee?"

"Maybe."

I showed him my ID. He scrutinized it carefully before handing it back.

"I'll take mine black," he said.

We picked up my bike at the gas station and I paid the guy the ten bucks I owed him. He came out and wanted to know what kind of bike it was that was worth twenty bucks to watch over. I told him it was stolen and he seemed suitably impressed. I fired it up, put on my helmet and snapped down the pillion pegs.

"Get on," I told Gary. "There's a coffee shop two blocks away."

He climbed aboard and I took it easy, mindful of the fact he wasn't wearing a helmet. I parked outside a late-night coffee shop, pulling in close so I could watch my bike from inside. It wasn't that busy and we took a booth by the window. I ordered coffee for both of us, black for Gary. After the waitress brought it over, Gary sat back in the booth and seemed to relax a little.

"I've heard your name around," he said, confirming that he was indeed an undercover cop.

"I made you back at Steve's," I told him.

"No way."

So I told him the giveaways. He was quiet for a while,

sipping his coffee.

"Jeez. I guess I do stand like that, too. That's a dead give-away."

"Only if you know what to look for," I told him. "So. Is Shriver under surveillance?"

He shook his head.

"He's low level. He pushes homemade dope. We're after much bigger fish. There's a bunch of crack houses out there." He pointed through the window, into the dark of the night. "Like to shut them down before they blow them-selves up. So, what's your beef with Shriver?"

I told him. Or at least, I gave him the outline. When I got to the last bit about engineering the fight, he laughed.

"You crazy bastard," he said. "You could have died back there, if any of his buddies had stepped in to lend a hand."

"True. But I was figuring you would step in and save the day."

"And blow my cover? In front of a hundred bikers? Your balls are bigger than your brains, pal."

Where've I heard that before?

We ordered a refill and I picked his brains about grow-ops. When he told me there were probably several thousand homes right here in Calgary being used to grow marijuana, I thought he was exaggerating. But he wasn't. And he might have been a little light, he said.

He told me how they run their operations, keeping the houses for about year.

"They buy them with little money down, using a fake buyer, then get them appraised for thirty or forty grand more than they are worth. They use the extra money to finance their grow-op. Afterwards, they'll often just burn the place down. Quicker than wiping up all the finger-prints."

In fifteen minutes, I got a detailed rundown on the grow-op problem in the city. By the time he'd finished, I could have started my own business. I knew it was bad. I just didn't know how bad.

When it was time to go, I paid the bill and scooped up my helmet.

"So, what happens if you don't manage to stop this fight?" he asked.

"I'm not sure. Why?"

Big grin.

"Can you get me tickets?"

Suddenly, everyone's a comedian.

Chapter Seventeen

THE NEXT MORNING, Cindy Palmer and I slept in. When I got home from Steve's place, I had taken a long, hot shower, swallowed a couple of Advil and a couple of Tylenol to help with the various swollen and painful bits, then waited until almost two before driving over to the Rocky View to pick up Cindy. I thought I had been moving smoothly but it didn't take her more than a few seconds to figure I wasn't. Besides, my lip was swollen.

"You've been fighting," she said as we headed to the parking lot.

"Which reminds me," I said, and passed her a five-dollar bill.

"What's this for?" she asked, taking it.

"Your winnings," I told her. "I placed a bet for you. A buck to win."

"At five to one? Which idiot gave those odds?"

"Me."

"What does the other guy look like?"

"He's probably over in Emerge having someone stitch

his lip. Do you want to go check?"

She didn't answer.

"Anyway, I won. And it wasn't really a fight. It was research."

"Is that what you call it?"

"Sure." I decided if I could confide in an undercover cop, I could confide in the woman I loved.

"You're such an idiot," she said afterwards, the words tinged with adoration and affection.

Well, tinged with not too much dislike.

"Give me back my five bucks," I said.

"What would happen if he'd beaten you?"

This was almost too easy.

"Then you'd owe me a buck," I said.

She tried not to laugh. But she was tired, and she was a nurse. And nurses have much the same twisted sense of humour as cops. She began to giggle.

"Tell me again why I go out with you?"

"Because I'm the only one who asked?"

"You're such a wiseass."

"Did you manage to dig up anything on you-know-who?" I asked.

"You-know-me," she said.

When we reached the Jimmy, she handed me a three-page computer printout. I scanned the private and confidential admissions information of one Ruby Shriver, born October 23, 1975.

"Jee-sus," I said, softly.

"Not exactly bedtime reading," she said.

"Fourteen broken bones?"

"She thinks by going to different hospitals, we won't figure it out."

"This thing is escalating," I said. Reading through the litany of beatings, it was obvious Ruby Shriver was in trouble. "There might not be a next time. This son of a bitch might kill her."

"Don't think *that* doesn't happen."

She didn't need to remind me of that. I folded the papers, put them away inside my jacket.

"I appreciate what you did, what you do for me, and I feel very bad for even asking you."

"But it's always for a good cause," she said.

"Always."

"When's the fight?"

I told her.

"Are we going?"

"I'm trying to stop it," I said, trying to keep my voice from spilling into incredulous. "It's not going to happen, Cin."

"But if it does, can you get tickets?"

I looked at her. She was quite beautiful. Tired as she was, her eyes were brilliant, her skin flawless, lips soft and full. So utterly feminine. Yet here she was, wanting to watch two grown men slug it out in a boxing ring. I'll never understand the fairer sex.

"Sure," I said.

"Ringside?"

"Where else?"

~

Sleeping in Cindy Palmer's bed was a rare pleasure. I only stayed over when Lindsay, her daughter, was away. Which wasn't often. But on those occasions, I enjoyed it thoroughly.

When I bought the new bike, courtesy of Danny's stock tips last year, I also splurged on Cindy Palmer. It wasn't difficult. She hardly ever spent anything on anything other than the necessities of life.

I'd invested seven grand. Seven months and three tips later, I cashed in thirty-six thousand dollars. I knew enough not to insult Danny with a cash bonus so I took him to dinner. He was very gracious and suggested I should buy something nice for Cindy because he's also a big fan. He suggested buying her something that she would never normally buy for herself.

My thoughts, exactly.

I bought her luxury items only. A top-of-the-line, king-size bed with a pillow-top mattress. Sexy bedsheets and down-filled pillows. And big, fluffy bath sheets that went around her twice. Or once, if I was in there with her. I bought her microwavable slippers. You heat them up, then slip your feet inside. It keeps them toasty warm for up to thirty minutes. Best of all, I bought her a folding massage table. Okay, maybe I bought that for me, but it came with a bag full of body oils and lotions and scented candles. I also hired a plumber to renovate her shower which now has multiple, adjustable showerheads on four vertical chrome columns. It's like standing in an Amazon rain forest. She loves it. I also bought her a flat screen television.

I'd tried to imagine what it must be like for her, on her feet in the ER for up to ten, sometimes twelve hours at a time, saving people's lives. Nurses work hard, particularly my nurse. She deserved to have as much relaxing luxury waiting for her when she got home as I could fit into her townhouse.

You cannot imagine how grateful she was.

Not to outdo myself, I bought a queen-size bed with the extra-thick pillow-top for my own place. It was guaranteed not to squeak, sag or otherwise show any signs of embarrassment.

Gymnastically speaking.

And if there's one area in which Cindy Palmer excels, particularly when she's happy, it's gymnastics.

I awoke next to her in her king-size bed a few minutes past nine. Large green eyes and a black nose were staring at me. I had a face full of fishy breath and hair on my tongue.

"Norman," I gagged. "Get your foot out my mouth."

Norman is Cindy's cat. She's a big, overly friendly female whose hormones run rampant twenty-four hours a day.

I showered in the main bathroom down the hall so I didn't disturb Cindy. Somewhere between shaving cream and shampoo, I reached a decision regarding the fight between Shriver and Paul Miller. Regardless of what Valerie Miller wanted, there was no way I could continue without telling her husband what he was getting himself into.

Even if I had to show him the bruises to prove it.

I counted at least two dozen. Mostly from the bare-knuckled body shots. They say it takes five days for the healing process to overtake the wounding process. Back in the mid-seventies, many American universities were spear-heading research into something called sensory deprivation.

Basically, they'd lock you up in a pitch-black, soundproofed room for the weekend. The idea was to reduce your sensory input to as close to zero as they could. When they did that, they discovered a very beneficial side effect. For instance, a couple of volunteer students had contracted poison ivy a few days earlier. Poison ivy has a shelf life of up to three weeks. So the powers-that-be decided to wrap the students' hands in layers of bandages to prevent them from scratching. Then they locked the students in separate sensory deprivation chambers and waited for the weekend to pass. Come Monday, when they let the students out, all signs of poison ivy had disappeared.

The scientists learned a valuable lesson. The brain, or perhaps more properly, the mind, is a very good healer. We just need to give it some space, some R&R time to do its job without all that other interference. When you're not feeling well, what do you do? You go to bed. You shut the drapes and turn off the lights (thereby reducing visual sensory input). You turn off the damned television, yell at the kids to shut up (now you're reducing auditory sensory input). You kick off the covers, stop eating, curl up into a fetal position and tell the world to leave you the hell alone (thereby reducing tactile stimulation.) You do all these things that are designed to reduce sensory input. The closer you can get to zero, the faster you'll heal. We already know this. But do we do it? Of course we don't. We soldier on, we go to the office when we're sick, we work through it, and we infect a few hundred other people, thereby prolonging the agony, ignoring the mind doctor who sits inside our heads.

Once I understood the process, I worked at isolating it. Now, when I hurt, I let my mind doctor do his thing.

Or maybe he's a she.

I'm nowhere near zero yet, but I'm maybe halfway. My bruising was already livid. It looked to be three, maybe four days old already. Ugly, discoloured bruising that had spread much farther than the initial point of impact. Within another two days, it would be gone. So I had to move rather quickly.

I phoned Valerie Miller shortly after my first coffee. I couldn't find any regular coffee in Cindy's kitchen, so I settled for a French vanilla blend. Sissy stuff that could get me disbarred from the Tough Guy club if anyone found out.

But boy, was it good. I'm thinking of getting some and repackaging it as Tough Guy's Kick-Ass Coffee.

It wasn't Valerie Miller who answered the phone, but her son, who was visiting his parents.

"Can I tell her who's calling?" he asked, though he didn't sound as if he cared much either way.

"Don King," I said.

She came on a minute later.

"Mr. King?"

"Good morning," I said.

"Good morning."

"We need to talk," I said.

"About what?"

I paused.

"You do know who this is?" I asked.

"Don King. Isn't it?"

"Do you even know who Don King is?"

"I'm talking with him, isn't that enough?"

"Actually, you're not," I said. "It's Eddie Dancer."

She paused.

"So who's Don King?"

"He's a really well-known fight promoter. His hair looks like a brush fire."

"Don't tell me he wants to promote this damn fight?"

Good grief.

"Well, no. I don't think this one's even on his radar."

"So, why are you calling me at home?"

"Because it's the only number I've got."

"Oh."

"And because we need to meet."

"When?"

"Today."

"Can't it wait?"

"Sure. But the longer you put it off, the worse it will get."

I could hear her brain cells colliding.

"Do you know where the Triplex is?"

"No."

She began to give me directions but I stopped her.

"When I said 'we' I meant the three of us."

"Which three?"

"You, me and Paul. I thought we should have a three-some. Preferably at your house."

"Why?"

Funny, she didn't query having a threesome.

"Because you both need to see me without my shirt on."

"I have a friend who'd enjoy this call a lot more than I am. Why don't I give you her number? You'd like her. She's a cougar."

A cougar?

"I'll pass. What time can I come out there?"

"You can't."

"I think the best way to stop this fight is to show your husband just how big a bite he's bitten off."

I wondered if I was mixing my metaphors.

She thought about it for long seconds.

"Oh, crap!"

"Is that a yes?"

She sighed. She really didn't like it when she didn't get her way.

"All right."

"I'll be there around —" I checked the time "— eleven-thirty."

"Oh, goody."

She hung up.

A cougar?

Huh!

Nurse Cindy would rip her apart and have the leftovers for breakfast.

Chapter Eighteen

THE HOUSE WAS LARGER than I expected. A towering two-storey that backed onto a manmade lake that would make a Texan laugh, slap his knee and tell you he'd spit bigger on his driest day. The front lobby was all dark hardwood, wrought-iron railings and artsy niches. I followed Valerie Miller through the house, detouring through the kitchen so she could refill her coffee and offer me one from a chromium monster sitting on a granite counter and spewing clouds of angry steam.

I declined.

Paul Miller was sitting in a room the realtor probably called the library, but which I'll call a cramped little room at the back of the house.

With a fireplace.

Correction.

A gas insert.

A pretend fireplace, and a small television with barely room for the remote on top. The television was on but the sound was turned all the way down.

He looked up from the sports section of the newspaper on his lap. Clearly, he wasn't expecting visitors. Valerie stood awkwardly, shuffling her feet. I stood next to her, wondering if this was one of my better ideas.

"Paul," she began, then ran out of things to say.

He sat, patiently waiting, looking from her to me, then back to his wife.

"Yes?"

"Paul, this is Mr. Dancer."

I'm so glad she didn't call me Eddie, because that might have implied a level of intimacy between us that I didn't feel existed. And Paul Miller was already looking at me somewhat suspiciously. He didn't bother shaking hands. Maybe the swollen lip made me look villainous.

"Yes?" was all he said.

Valerie Miller looked to me to carry the conversation from there. I decided this would go down better if I were seated. I chose a little black leather number across from Paul, since it was the only other chair in the room.

"Mr. Miller," I began. "I'm a private detective." I let that sink in while his mind ran through myriad possibilities. If he was having an affair, he concealed it well.

He folded his paper and laid it aside.

"So?"

"Your wife asked my advice about something."

He glanced at Valerie, but she was giving up nothing. Old Velcro-lips Val.

I considered him before I answered. He was sitting down, so it was hard to estimate his full height, but I'd guess around five-nine, five-ten. And he was carrying a little gut, not much, maybe an extra ten or fifteen pounds, which would put him around one-ninety. The wounds he'd taken to his head were pretty much healed. His hair was growing back but I could see a few angry red lines when he turned to look at his wife. He turned back to me.

"You mind telling me what this is about?" he asked. He was getting impatient and I knew the next sentence would be, "Or get the hell out of my house."

"Victor Shriver."

He blinked once before turning to look at Valerie. I could see he was upset.

"That's not up for discussion," was all he said.

"Let me ask you something, Mr. Miller. What are you doing to prepare for the fight?"

"None of your business."

"Because you should be out there —" I pointed to the great outdoors "— running wind sprints, building aerobic endurance, losing ten or fifteen pounds and replacing that loss with solid new muscle. You should have a strength trainer, a coach, a fight trainer, a fight doctor and half a dozen sparring partners. You should be booking time in a gym, time on the speed bag and the heavy bag. You should be jumping rope, doing crunches, building up your resistance to getting smacked, repeatedly, in the solar plexus. And on the chin."

He watched me the whole time without interrupting.

"Because if you don't do all these thing, Mr. Miller, if you cheat yourself out of even one of them, the day you step into that ring may well be your last."

A terrible, truthful silence filled the empty space that

the Millers called the library.

"I appreciate your concern —" and here he meant the two of us "— but I can handle the likes of Victor Shriver, thank you all the same."

I sighed. I knew it would come to this. I stood up, unzipped my jacket, shrugged it off and pulled my shirt out of my pants.

"What are you doing?" He sat forward as if to stop me.

"Look," I said.

I pulled my shirt over my head and dropped it on the floor. I turned first left, then right, the better to show him the bruises.

Valerie Miller gasped.

But that might have been my physique.

"Jesus," he said.

He looked pale.

"Victor Shriver did this," I said. "I'm supposed to know how to handle myself. Do you still think you can handle him?"

"Oh, Paul."

Valerie Miller looked terrified. Paul Miller looked unsettled.

"God, Paul. He'll kill you."

"Why did he do this?" Paul asked me.

I decided that honesty was the best policy.

"Because your wife asked me to see if the fight could be stopped," I told him. "Now they are selling tickets, Paul. Fifty and one hundred bucks a pop. All told, stopping the fight could cost in excess of twenty-five-thousand dollars. I decided to find out what you'd gotten yourself into, to find

out if Shriver was all balls and Brylcreem, or if he was real."
I paused. "I'm here to tell you, Paul, he's the real meal deal."

Valerie stared down at her husband.

"I'm scared," she said. "I'm too damned young to be a widow."

I saw something pass across his eyes then, or maybe it passed behind them. It was a look I'd seen before. And I knew, as rattled as he was, Paul Miller wasn't about to back down. He'd made his bed, and as sure as God made little apples, he was going to lie in it.

"We'll talk about this later," he said.

I picked up my shirt and put it back on. As I turned to leave, I picked up the TV remote.

"I think there's a boxing match on TSN," I said and tossed him the remote.

He caught it with his left hand.

Which was the only bit of good news all morning.

Chapter Nineteen

SHE WAS BACK THE VERY NEXT morning. I looked up from behind my desk.

"Good morning," I said.

She sat down hard in the same chair she sat in the first time she came to visit me. This time, she looked tired.

"He isn't going to stop," she said.

"I guessed he wasn't."

"Really?"

"Yes. When he makes his mind up about something, he sees it through."

She looked a bit puzzled.

"How could you know that?"

I shrugged.

"I've seen the look before."

"Well, he said to tell you he appreciates your concern, but he's still going ahead with the fight." She suddenly looked real sore. "Especially after your visit. All that crap about gyms and wind sprints and stuff. Now he's out there looking for a personal trainer."

Oops.

"That might not necessarily be a bad thing," I said.

"Really?" she said, peeling the paintwork.

"I mean, *if* he does step into that ring, he needs to be prepared."

"It's not *if*. It's when. His mind's made up." She began to fidget. "And if Asshole can work you over like that, what chance has Paul got?"

"Last night was research," I told her, my pride wounded. "If we'd had a real fight, Mr. Shriver would be breathing through a tube."

"Oh."

She sat in silence for a few moments.

"Don't get me wrong," I said. "Your husband's still in serious trouble."

"I know that."

Here it comes.

"That's why I want to hire you to help train him."

What did I tell you?

Chapter Twenty

HE WASN'T HAPPY. I guess he had every right not to be, considering his wife had snuck behind his back and hired me to stop his fight. But, as I pointed out to him, she did it with the best of intentions.

"With which, the road to hell is paved," he reminded me.

"You've every right to be pissed," I told him. We were sitting in his library again, just the two of us this time. "Now, if I can get you to channel that anger in the right direction, you *might* walk away from this thing intact."

Listen to me.

God forbid, I could get a job in advertising.

"And you can help me do that how?"

"Well, let's review the Marquis of Queensberry Rules," I said.

"Why?"

"I feel it's important that at least one of you has a passing acquaintance with their existence. And it might as well be you because it sure as hell ain't Victor Shriver."

He shrugged a go-ahead.

"Okay. There are twelve rules."

"Is that all?"

"It'll go quicker if you don't interrupt."

"Sure. Anything that gets you out of here faster."

"They were drawn up back in the eighteen-hundreds. Eighteen sixty-five," I said, showing off a little. "They were designed to persuade boxers —" I added air quotes "— not to fight simply to win, but win by following the rules. And if you think Shriver's going to follow them, remind me to talk to you about a real estate opportunity in southern Florida."

"What are you saying?"

"You need a trainer who knows the rules," I said, "and one who doesn't give a damn."

"But there's to be a referee," he said.

"Sure there is."

"Who's impartial."

"Which will be of great comfort to you while you're in a coma, or when he rips your ear off with his teeth or bursts an eardrum, or delivers a rip that requires you to pee in a bag for three months, or when he cracks your windpipe open, or gouges out one of your eyes, or both of them. All of which have happened under the impartial noses of trained referees. Face it, Paul. This isn't a boxing match. It's a slugfest. And if you plan on boxing him while he plans on slugging you to death, the smart money's going south."

He stared at his feet for an inordinate amount of time before finally looking up.

"All right," he said. "You win. When do we start?"

I shot a cuff, checked my watch.

"How's now?"

~

There was really only one trainer who would even consider such a foolhardy venture. Fortunately, he was the only one I wanted. His name was Bert Fagnall. And if you think he hasn't heard every gay joke about his last name, think again. He's sixty-something and has spent every day of his life, since he was nine years old, hanging around gyms, and I don't mean the pretty ones that have Ladies Nite every Tuesday and Thursday. I mean real gyms where real men bleed. Where weightlifting means exactly that. Where the boxing ring is the shrine and men of all ages worship through pints of blood, sweat and tears. Bert Fagnall, an official senior citizen, still climbs between the ropes every day, dons his headgear and a pair of blocker pads and works kids less than a third of his age into sweaty submission. He's built like a grizzly bear. His shoulders have no beginning, they have no end. They are wide enough to require their own postal code. If he were ever to straighten up, his shadow would plunge the entire city into deep, dark shadows. He doesn't speak so much as mumble or growl. He's a gruff, bluff, short-tempered pain in the ass and he's still the best damned trainer in North America. He owns a gym in Ogden, in Calgary's industrial southeast, near the rail yards. It's a walk-up. He has three boxing rings, umpteen body bags, speed bags and skipping ropes. The wooden floor is made of barn board that's so dark it seems to absorb every bit of light in the place. He's open seven days a week, from five in the morning until ten o'clock at night. If you're young, show promise and can't afford the membership fees, he'll hire you to keep the place shipshape, and he'll work you to death, both in the ring and out of it.

He has the respect of countless boxers of all ages and doesn't give a rip what any other human being on God's earth thinks about him, and he's worn the same damned cardigan every day for the past ten years.

I think it's dark blue.

I'd struck a deal with the Millers. I refunded over half the fee that Valerie had paid me. They would use the refund to pay Bert, plus whatever else it cost to use his facilities and his services until the fight. In turn, Bert agreed to train Paul. He'd agreed to put Paul in the ring with sparring partners, to make him work the bags, to sweat fifteen pounds of fat from his bones and hang muscle in places he never knew he had. I didn't ask Paul how this would interfere with his job search. He made a commitment, and I fully expected him to renege before the end of the first week. The sheer brutality of such a physical pace would weaken his resolve immediately.

I'd packed shorts, runners, an old T-shirt, a couple of bath towels and a full case of bottled water. I told Paul to bring pretty much the same. I was surprised when he showed in Valerie's Lexus, with Valerie in the passenger seat.

"Any trouble finding the place?" I asked.

He patted the dash.

"GPS," he said.

Pity they couldn't build it into his boxing gloves. I figured he'd need such a miracle to find Shriver's chin.

The gym entrance was located around back and above a row of specialty stores. Well, *specialty stores* might give the wrong impression. They were stores that sold everything from recycled car parts to reconditioned vacuum cleaners to used DVDs, and *sold* was a tad misleading. Maybe *fenced* was more appropriate, and used DVDs implied some artistic content; not a chance. Everything sold down here was for an adult audience. Funny how that term immediately precludes artistic merit of any kind.

I locked the Jimmy, set the alarm and dropped Bert's business card face-up on the dash. It was almost a certainty that nobody would touch the truck, since most people either respected Bert too much to steal from his patrons or were scared to death of him.

We climbed the outside wooden staircase. It had needed a few licks of paint when I was there last year. Now it needed a few cans. The stairs led to a covered porch with a heavy green metal door that opened straight into the gym. I pushed it open, and Paul and Valerie Miller followed me inside.

The place was gloomy. Not dark, just gloomy, as every other overhead light bulb was missing. That was because Bert Fagnall is a miserly old bastard.

The room was long and narrow. To the right, racks of free weights lined the wall. On the opposite side ran a seventy-foot run of floor-to-ceiling mirrors. Between the weight racks stood maybe two dozen workbenches. There were no weight machines in Bert's gym. He hated them. He'd seen his fair share of pretty-boy boxers over the years, boxers who'd worked with machines to bulk up, and I'd first heard the phrase, "Body by Nautilus, brains by Mattel" in Bert's gym. Word quickly spread that Bert was a free-weights freak.

No matter when you came, Bert's place was always busy,

and the clientele was eclectic, a rare mix of young, old and everywhere in-between. While Bert steadfastly refused to train women, there was still no shortage of the fairer sex who enjoyed working with free weights and kicking the crap out of the heavy bags.

We changed in what used to be Bert's office. It was the only changing room and we followed the ladies first rule and let Valerie change into her gym gear before we changed into ours.

"I've decided to quit smoking," she said when we came out, and Paul rolled his eyes.

"You've quit before?" I asked.

"A time or two," she admitted. "But this time it's different."

"How so?" Paul asked.

"All those other times, I kept a pack of cigarettes in my purse. This time, I'm flying solo."

"Good for you," I said, secretly thinking I should stay at least a hundred yards from her at all times.

We found Bert Fagnall in the far ring. A hulking figure, shambling around in carpet slippers and sweatpants topped by the aging cardigan. The inevitable cigarette hung from nicotine-stained lips. Bert was holding a mismatched pair of blocking pads in front of his upper body. As he shuffled in a circle, a gangly kid in his late teens tried to punch the life out of him.

"Jab!" Bert growled, and the kid shot a straight left at the right-hand blocker.

Bert brushed him away with practiced ease.

"Again. Put some guts into it."

The kid stepped into the next jab, and Bert swatted him

away. The kid got his feet tangled because he'd stepped off on the wrong foot. He fell hard and took most of the impact on his elbows.

Bert stopped, shook his head, dropped his guard.

"Hit the showers, kid," he growled.

Which was Bert's little joke, since there weren't any. He came towards us and hung over the top rope. It sagged, in danger of dumping him clean out of the ring, but Bert just hung there, in defiance of the laws of gravity.

"Eddie!"

What passed for a smile crossed his lips and I introduced him to Paul and Valerie Miller. I'd explained the situation in detail on the phone. Bert pulled his right hand free of the blocker, stuck his arm through the space between the top two ropes, and shook hands with Paul. He didn't bother shaking hands with Valerie, giving her a curt nod instead.

I helped Paul into the ring. I'd already taped his hands and picked a pair of worn leather sparring gloves from one of several boxes in the far corner. Paul stood, looking out of place, his arms hanging long, like a forlorn ape, unsure what was happening to him.

"Paul's a southpaw," I told Bert.

"That right?" Bert squinted around the plume of cigarette smoke that made his left eye water. He turned to Paul. "You a southpaw?"

"What's a southpaw?" Paul asked and Bert looked at me over his shoulder.

"After I'm all finished with Rocky," he said, "I'll walk on water."

"That I'd like to see," I said.

I guided Valerie away from the ring. The next hour was going to be ugly. I took her down the gym to the free weights and asked her if she'd ever used them before.

"Do cans count?" she asked.

"Cans?"

"Yes. Food cans. I used to do arm curls with cans of beans, tins of peaches, stuff like that."

I thought about it for a moment.

"I don't think that counts," I told her.

"Then no."

"Okay. What do you want to achieve?"

"Muscle tone."

A kid, ripped on steroids, shuffled past.

"But I don't what to look like *that*," she added, loud enough for him to hear.

"You won't," I assured her.

I started her out on a full-body program using free weights to strengthen her core muscles. The only thing approaching state-of-the-art that Bert had bought in the last ten years was a pair of BOSU balls, half-balls on a flat plastic base that helped build and strengthen the core muscles and improved a person's balance. I made her stand on a BOSU ball while she worked with the various weights.

Val seemed to enjoy herself, but every few minutes she'd stop and watch Paul, who was dragging himself around the ring, flailing wildly in pursuit of Bert, who appeared light on his feet and positively nimble compared to her husband. Bert would mutter words of encouragement — at least, I suspect that's what she hoped he was doing. Paul's T-shirt was dark with sweat.

When the hour with the free weights was over, I left her and spent some time on the speed bag, building a rhythm before picking up the pace. I thought about Danny Many-Guns. If I impressed Valerie Miller on the speed bag, she should watch Danny. He did it with his eyes closed, using the backs of his knuckles, barely brushing the leather, building his rhythms quickly until the bag and his hands were a blur, an almost continuous single visual. And the sound: not the drumbeat, machine-gun staccato blast I had trouble maintaining, but a pure sound that seemed to have no breaks in it.

By the time I'd finished, Paul was out of the ring. He was sitting on a long wooden bench, shoulders slumped, hands hanging between his knees, gloves resting on the floor. He was breathing hard through his mouth.

"You want the good news or the bad news?" Bert asked me.

"Give me the bad news," I said. "I'm sick of good news today."

"He's only got one punch," Bert said.

I looked over at Paul. He was heavy through the shoulders and I'd been watching him surreptitiously for the past hour.

"Lemme guess," I said. "A left hook?"

"He's only got the hook, but he can throw it from the left or the right. Which is the good news."

You take good news where you find it.

"Can you add an uppercut?"

"He has rotator cuff issues. Both shoulders."

"Would physio help?"

"Not enough time."

"How about working on his jab?"

"Same problem. This guy threw a lot of baseballs in his prime. I'm surprised he's got the power he's got in his hook."

Not good news. If he only had a hook, that meant he had to fight inside. No one could throw a hook, left or right or otherwise, if he was standing outside his opponent's guard. Fighters had to go toe-to-toe.

And Shriver could switch-hit from an innie to an outie to a brawler as the mood took him.

All in all, not a very auspicious beginning.

Even for a southpaw.

Chapter Twenty-One

EIGHT WEEKS ISN'T VERY LONG to train a boxer for a major fight. To take a guy who's never boxed, who's in hopeless shape to begin with, and to expect to turn him into some sort of prizefighter in that same time period is a pie-in-the-sky impossibility. The best we could hope for was that he'd drop a dozen pounds, add some muscle, particularly around the solar plexus, and learn to throw a few punches.

And to block any incoming punches that might put him on his ass in the first round.

Or put him in hospital.

Or worse. Put him in the morgue.

And we needed some secret intelligence. Some ground-level spies who could report on progress in the Shriver camp.

Since my mug was known around Workouts, clearly I couldn't spy on Shriver's training. And even if they let me in, I hardly thought Shriver himself would allow me to stand around and watch him in the ring. No, it had to be someone they'd never seen before. Someone they'd never suspect as being from the Miller camp.

And I knew exactly who could pull it off.

My old mates, Nosher and Splosher.

They had moved, last year, to a much larger acreage. They had, I think, twenty acres southwest of Millarville. God's country, since God was the only one who could afford the land prices. The Municipal District of Foothills covers an area of roughly fourteen hundred square miles south of Calgary. The price of land within the Foothills MD varies tremendously, depending on how many acres you buy and where those acres are located. You can buy a quarter section of raw farmland, which is a hundred and sixty acres, for about half a million dollars. Or you can buy a secluded, three-acre parcel with stunning mountain views for about the same amount of money.

All I can say is, I'm glad I'm not in real estate.

I phoned ahead and Nosher answered.

Or maybe it was Splosher.

It's hard to tell with identical twins. They came by their respective nicknames honestly enough.

Actually, they didn't.

They came by their names as a result of a very dishonest practice, back in the U.K. from whence they came, of fixing up old cars, usually much-sought-after red, two-seater MG TDS, with baling wire and duct tape (an art form known as "noshing") and repainting over dodgy bodywork with a hard-drying lacquer that looked fabulous for all of a month (otherwise known as "sploshing") until their luck ran out.

And so did they.

They arrived in Canada a number of years ago and have

been working hard at going straight ever since.

Well, one can always hope.

I rode out to see them. It's blacktop all the way to their drive, after which it's two hundred yards of deep gravel. I stayed in second gear and rode the gravel with my legs out, like a pair of training wheels. The secret to riding on gravel is the same as riding on sand. You let the bike decide where to go and you go along for the ride. If you try and outmuscle the gravel, it will think you want to arm-wrestle.

And you'll lose.

I parked on the concrete apron in front of their garage. They had bought what the Americans call a rancher, but Canadians call it a bungalow with a front veranda. Nosher was sitting on the veranda with his feet up on the rail, drinking what might have been coffee.

Or it might have been a rum punch.

Hard to tell.

Beatrice, their hefty excuse for a guard dog, lay on her belly and eyed me with suspicion. She was a black Newfie cross with a bad hip. Newfies are generally good-natured, and Beatrice was too. It's just that whenever she gave in to her friendly nature, the twins would berate her, telling her to attack the intruder and not to make nice. I squatted beside her and rubbed her ears, which got her tail going, which in turn tipped her over onto her back, legs sticking straight up like she'd died and rigor mortis had set in. Her wet, pink tongue fell out of her mouth and she entered the Kingdom of Heaven upside down and drooling.

We should all be so lucky.

"S'up, bro?" Nosher called from the deck.

I joined him, my boots making a nice loud clumping noise on the deck wood. I pulled a spare Adirondack chair alongside his and sat down next to him.

It didn't take long to explain what I wanted.

"Why don't we take this arsehole outta the picture?" he said.

"If you do, it will only delay things," I said. "Paul Miller is driven to fight this man."

He thought about that. You could see he was disappointed not to lay a beating on a guy who knocked his wife around.

"Maybe after the fight is over?" he said.

"Sure." I could see that. "On your own time, you guys can do whatever you want. Only you might have to take a number."

"Oh. Right. You and Danny are next in line, then?"

"Something like that," I said.

I hadn't told him that Danny wasn't on the job. The twins knew nothing about Danny's life before they met him. No point opening up that can of worms today.

"Where's Splosh?"

"Ha! You know he had that heart thing?"

"What heart thing?"

"He thought his ticker was giving up," Nosher said. "Got in a real tizz. Turned out it was just a virus or something. Anyway, he decided he needed to get into shape. And you know Splosher. Never does nothing by halves."

Which was true of both of them.

"So where is he?" I asked again.

He dropped his feet off the deck rail. Beatrice looked up a moment, then let her shaggy head drop back onto her paws.

"Come on," he said. "Y'ain't gonna believe this without seeing it."

I followed him over to the barn. It was huge. Maybe a hundred feet deep and seventy feet wide. And high. It stood a good twenty feet at the eaves. I wondered why they needed something so big when they bought the place. It had stayed empty the whole of last year, as far as I knew.

We came to the man-door on the north end.

"You ready for this?" he said.

I could hear the rhythmic thumping of a bass coming from inside. Nosher pulled open the door and gave an exaggerated bow as he waved me inside. The music was loud. I recognized the song.

It was "Black Betty," by the Ram Jams.

But it wasn't the music that held my attention.

I stood inside the entrance, totally baffled by what I was looking at. Even now, I'm still not sure I can adequately describe it. Splosher had filled the inside of the cavernous barn with staircases. There were hundreds of them. As my eyes grew somewhat accustomed to the sight, I realized each staircase was attached to another staircase. Directly in front of me, a wooden staircase rose up ten feet. At the top, a short, flat walkway connected it to another staircase that dropped down to the floor. There, it connected to a long, narrow staircase that went up almost to the roofline. Another walkway connected to another staircase, this one at a ninety-degree angle, that dropped down to be lost in a jumble of treads and railings and walkways, as far as the eye could see in every direction.

"What the hell is this?" I asked Nosher.

"It were Splosher's idea. He picked up . . . oops."

I waited but he didn't explain the oops. I turned to face him.

"Oops what?"

"Nothing."

"Nosher, what did you do?"

"I forgot about the door."

"What about it?"

I'd have an easier time pulling wisdom teeth.

"It only has one handle. On the outside. So once he's in, he's committed."

"To what?"

"To climbing the Empire State Building."

"The what?"

"That's how many stairs there are."

"And the only way out was through that door?"

"Right."

I looked at my feet. I was wearing my Alpinestar boots. Great for gravel. Not so great for climbing the Empire State Building.

"You're sure about this?" I asked him.

"I hung the bleedin' door. Trust me. There's only one way out."

I sighed.

"Never a dull moment."

I sat down and took my boots off. I left them beside the handleless door, and we both began the arduous climb.

"How many stairs are there?"

"I forget. It's about thirty-seven hundred and sommat."

He bumped into me when I stopped. I turned and looked

at him but I could see he was serious.

"That heart thing gave Splosher a real scare," Nosher said. "He hates jogging, hates getting on the treadmill, and you can't get him in a swimming pool neither. His doctor told him he needed to do some cardio, so he came up with this."

"Have you never heard of a StairMaster?"

"A what?"

"Never mind."

"Most of this was bankrupt stock," he said.

Which meant at least half of it had been nicked. I wondered how many two-storey homes around Calgary were missing a staircase.

"Three thousand seven hundred stairs seems a lot," I said.

"Yeah, it is. It's twice as many as in the Empire State Building."

That stopped me.

"Twice?"

"Yeah. Well, he figured there was no point putting in the same amount."

"Why not?"

We were on our sixth staircase. I wondered how many hundreds we had left.

"Think about it, Eddie. If you're going to climb to the top of the Empire State Building, how you gonna get back down?"

The elevator?

"He put in double the number. There's eighteen hundred and sixty odd going up, and eighteen hundred and sixty odd going down. You got to give Splosher his due, Eddie. He's thorough."

Hardly the word I would have used.

It took us an hour to climb the Empire State Building. By which time, the soles of my socks were wearing thin and I'd worked up a sweat that made my leather pants creak with every step up. And down.

We caught glimpses of Splosher occasionally. He'd yell encouragement over the music, waving at us through the vertical and horizontal bits of wood as he pounded up or down a flight of stairs. Once, we even passed each other, as people do when they're shopping in department stores, travelling between floors on the escalators.

Eventually, I began to enjoy it. I've never been one to shirk a sweaty workout. Then I began to wonder if they might not have a brilliant idea here. They could franchise them. Open up "Stairway To Heaven" clubs all across North America. People would love them. Especially the handleless door idea.

It beat the boredom of a StairMaster, for sure.

I sent Nosher back for my boots and afterwards, we sat out on the deck and drank cold beer. I felt I'd earned mine. I listened while Nosher told Splosher what I needed them for, and Splosher was quick to climb aboard.

"You think he'd want to use my stairs?" Splosher asked.

I'd thought about it, but it was too far out and Paul could get in an hour or two of extra wind sprints in the time it took to get here.

"Fair enough." Splosher went back to his beer.

"Do we get reimbursed?" Nosher asked. "For the gym membership?"

I agreed, of course, to cover all their costs, and they celebrated with another beer. Beatrice came over and rested her head on my foot. The sun baked down on us. Bumblebees droned happily in the distance. Somewhere, a long way off, a tractor chugged across an unplowed field. I was beginning to understand the attraction of acreage living. I wondered what my little house in Marde Loop might fetch.

"Crap."

It was Nosher. He'd been inside to use the bathroom.

"The bloody septic's backed up again. The damn bathroom's flooded."

Pop!

That bubble burst.

I left them then, and headed back to city plumbing and civilization as fast as my bike would take me.

Which was astonishingly fast.

Chapter Twenty-Two

I KEPT IN TOUCH WITH Bert Fagnall and watched the weeks fly by. Bert phoned me with regular updates, as did the twins. Bert's reports were never as encouraging as I might have hoped. The twins had even less to report. Victor Shriver's training seemed sporadic, at best. Which was a good sign. Except that, on those occasions he did show up to train, he beat the snot out of his sparring partners. And sparring partners were hard to come by. The best sparring partners would have been southpaws, like Paul, because they keep a boxer sharp and on his game. But southpaws are hard to come by, and Shriver had to settle for what the gym could find him, which tended to be rookies, some still fresh out of high school.

Over the next month, I became sidetracked with other jobs, new clients who demanded, and deserved, my undivided time and attention. I received the odd call from Valerie Miller but never from Paul himself. She remained necessarily optimistic that Paul was making solid progress. Since my late-night coffee meeting with Gary Vaughan, the undercover cop, I had always intended to pursue another angle with the Shrivers. I believed if it were Victor Shriver who had to cancel and not Paul Miller, it might eliminate the Millers' responsibility to pay any cancellation fees. Gary believed Victor Shriver was selling homemade pot, and I had a pretty good idea where the Shrivers were growing it.

With less than three weeks left before fight night, I finally found time to make the return trip to the Shrivers' acreage. Mother Nature had made some changes. The ground was warm and fertile and the prairie grasses grew tall and wild. I arrived early, around five in the morning, and had to search hard for the overgrown gully I'd used the last time. I brought a variety of supplies with me, including my camera, binoculars, food and water. I lay beneath an earth-tone blanket, and covered it with loose dirt from the edges of the gully. I might be there for three or four days and needed to be well-concealed. I remembered to turn off the ringer of my cell phone and set it on vibrate.

I'd finally, reluctantly, asked Danny for help.

I'd outlined the case briefly, and told him I needed a ride. And later, I would need picking up. He never complained, even though he had to get up at some ridiculous hour to pick me up from my house at four in the morning and drop me off half a mile from the Shrivers' acreage.

I think he sensed that there was more to this case than simply training Paul Miller to become an amateur boxer. But he never asked, never voiced his concerns.

Much of my plan depended on making friends with Brutus, and I had packed a large piece of raw, juicy beef for him. I had everything in two backpacks. One was full of bottled water, the second, mainly food. I planned on eating nothing but protein. Protein produces little, if any, waste. Once I was dug in, I didn't want to disturb my hide with constant bathroom breaks.

Brutus was still chained to the stake in the front yard. He looked thinner and paid me no interest, though I was pretty sure he could hear me. I think he was simply too hot, lying without shade in direct sunlight, even that early in the morning. And it was hot. Within minutes, I had a swarm of flies circling my head. I dug a narrow trench for my elbows, propped the camera and binoculars in front of me, and waited for the world around me to come to life.

Day One was a sweaty blur. I took several shots of Victor Shriver and his father, Roy, as they trekked between the barn and their respective trailers. It was the barn that interested me. Through my binoculars, I observed that the barn door was a heavy metal affair with a padlock strung through a length of heavy-duty chain. The last man out of the barn never failed to lock it securely behind him.

During the first two days, I watched as they took turns working in the barn. Roy Shriver worked the night shift. He came out around six-thirty in the morning, and Victor went in around seven-thirty. The old man sat around for a couple of hours, knocking back half a dozen beers on his deck before calling it quits. I wondered if he had running water in his trailer, for he never bothered using the plumbing. When Mother Nature called, he simply stood on the edge of the deck and peed into the dying yellow grass. His trailer must have been hotter than a breadbox but it didn't seem to bother him. When he stepped inside on the first day, I saw the drapes move in the end room, the one far-thest from the barn, and figured that was his bedroom. With the beer, the heat and the all-nighter in the barn, I guessed he'd pretty much sleep the day away.

Victor came and went. He'd spend an hour or two in the barn, then he'd drive off somewhere for an hour, some-times longer. When he came back, he always headed straight to the barn, never to his trailer. He'd rummage in the trunk of the car, then carry some supplies to the barn.

I saw Ruby, too. She'd step out and hang baby clothes on the line, take other stuff down. Three times a day she'd carry food down to Brutus. He'd watch her, his tail stirring up dust motes. He seemed listless but always managed to shake off his lethargy when she put the food down in front of him. She filled his water bowl and stroked his massive head while he ate. Other than that, he received no attention the whole time I was there.

Between sightings, I scanned the roofline of the barn and counted eight exhaust vents that should not have been there. Growing pot produces a tremendous amount of odour and moisture, and both must be vented outside or the moisture will quickly seep into exposed wood. Once the moisture content in the wood exceeds twenty percent, it sets up an ideal environment for mould. And once mould begins to grow, it spreads like wildfire and destroys the very wood that spawns it.

Before Day Two dawned, while Roy Shriver was in the barn, I cut a piece of raw meat for Brutus. If his hearing was a little impaired, there was nothing wrong with his nose. I'd barely put the motherlode away before his head rose in the moonlight. I could hear him sniffing. I cut the piece in sugar-cube chunks and whispered his name. I could see him clearly, a dark shadow against the baked earth. I threw the meat underarm, landing it well within the circle of his chain.

He gobbled it up in seconds.

I threw three more pieces, all within his reach. I had his undivided attention.

"Good boy," I whispered to him in the 3 a.m. darkness, and he watched me alertly as I moved down the slope towards him. I tossed two more pieces and watched him devour them. I squatted at the edge of the circle, maybe two feet beyond his reach.

He growled, low in the chest.

"Good boy, Brutus." I spoke softly and threw another cube of beef at his feet.

He ignored it, continuing to growl quietly at me.

"Bye."

I moved back, and he stopped growling. He sucked up the meat at his feet and came over to the edge of the circle, dragging the chain behind him. I stayed where I was, cut another piece of meat and tossed it to him. This time he caught it in mid-air.

"Good boy, Brutus!" I whispered.

He caught the next three pieces and I saw his tail wagging in the moonlight. Time to see if he was ready to make friends. I moved closer. Instead of backing up or barking, he began to wiggle his bum, getting silly. I held out another piece, and he took it gently from my outstretched hand. I let him sniff me, then began rubbing him gently with the back of my hand. Starved for affection, he didn't take long to accept me as his new best friend. He slid down my leg, hit the ground, and rolled onto his back. I rubbed his chest and raked my nails across the dry, matted fur of his belly. His tongue lolled and he stretched out, his legs clawing thin air. He was in doggy heaven.

I kept it up for fifteen minutes. Then I gave him the rest of the cut meat and put my face against his snout. He licked my face, my ears, my neck. When I was sure he had my scent, I pushed him away, told him to lie down. At first, he was reluctant to move, but I spoke softly to him again and this time he did as he was told. He went to the small depression he'd made in the ground and circled around three times before curling into a tight ball.

"There's a good Brutus."

I moved up the slope and rearranged my hide. By the time Roy Shriver came out of the barn at six-thirty, I was invisible and Brutus was sleeping like a well-fed baby.

Chapter Twenty-Three

ON THE THIRD DAY, things took a nasty turn.

It was around nine-thirty that morning when Victor came out of the barn, banging the door shut behind him. Roy Shriver drained the last of a six-pack on the deck of his trailer. He looked up at Victor, and I fired off three quick shots on auto-focus.

"What's your goddamned problem?" Roy yelled.

Victor looked angry. He kicked at a stone, sending it skimming off into the long grass before answering.

"That fuckin' row of lights burned out again!"

"Thought you'd fixed that?"

"Yeah. So did I. I tol' you we got too fuckin' many on that circuit. Now I gotta go get a whole new set."

"Watch your mouth, boy." It was a low, mean warning and he hawked up a wad of phlegm and spat it out over the porch rail for additional emphasis.

Victor stood with his head on his chest, casting a long shadow, and I aimed the camera at him and captured three more pictures.

"I gotta go to Calgary," he said. "Somewhere's I ain't been before. Maybe the north end." Then he looked up at the old man. "I need cash money," he said.

"Wha —?"

"I need cash."

Roy Shriver sat looking at him a long moment. Then he scrunched the beer can in his hand and stood up so fast, he knocked his chair over. The falling chair made Brutus jump. He scurried away quickly as the old man threw the empty beer can at him but missed.

He turned and bashed open the trailer door, returning a minute later with a fistful of bills. Victor hadn't moved.

He held the money out. Victor walked over and took it. Again, I caught their digital image. Victor put the money in his pocket without counting it, crossed the yard and locked the barn door with the heavy padlock. He wore the key on a cord around his neck, the same as his father. Then he walked to the aging Granada. He opened the driver's door and stood a while, letting the heat out before he slid behind the wheel. Roy Shriver watched him disappear down the drive, then he turned and walked back inside his trailer.

A little later, Ruby came out of her trailer. She carried a bowl of water in one hand and a bowl of scraps in the other.

"Brutus!"

She put the bowls down carefully just inside the circle. Brutus came over and drank half the water in one go. I took the time to focus and got some good close-ups. Ruby stayed put, squatting beside the dog, stroking his head absentmindedly in the hot sun. Neither she nor Brutus noticed Roy Shriver step out of the trailer in his stockinged feet.

He stood watching Ruby's back for a few moments before adjusting his crotch, an obscene gesture because his hand lingered and he made a series of long, stroking gestures. When he moved, he did it slowly, deliberately, coming up behind her like a ghost. At the last minute, Brutus saw him and spooked, shifting quickly away. Ruby tried to stand but Shriver was too fast for her. He wrapped his arms around her thin body, lifting her clean off the ground as he spun her in a full circle, dropping her to her feet well outside the chain circle. She struggled, and Shriver made a nasty noise that was somewhere between a laugh and a bark. I watched as he reached up and cupped her breasts between his hands, squeezing them as he buried his mouth in the nape of her neck. She stiffened, her whole body tensing up. I caught it all with the camera and I was pretty sure Ruby wasn't enjoying any of it.

I know I wasn't.

In one fast movement, he pulled the front of her dress up over her waist and jammed his other hand down the front of her panties, his fingers clawing at her, forcing his way inside. She cried out, not from passion, but from fear and pain and a deep humiliation. His hands were dirty, the nails black with crusted dirt.

I threw off the blanket and got my feet under me, starting down the slope towards him, when a phone suddenly rang loudly, the bell outside in the yard. I stopped, dropped in a crouch and watched him. He reacted in a burst of temper, spinning Ruby roughly around and cuffing her across the head before pushing her away. She lost a shoe, tripped and fell sideways, scrambled away from him and got back on her feet as he walked quickly to the trailer. As he stepped up onto the deck, he turned and placed the fingers of his left hand under his nose, sniffing her scent and sneering at her as he did so.

It turned my stomach.

I could only wonder how Ruby felt.

Then he stepped inside the trailer and slammed the door shut behind him.

She collected her shoe and carried it to her trailer. It was hard to tell if she was even crying.

Neither of them had noticed me crouching fifty feet from them, ready to tear Roy Shriver to pieces and to feed his bloody remains to Brutus.

Chapter Twenty-Four

I WENT BACK TO MY HIDE and waited. I was angry and it took a long time to get it under control. An hour passed and there was no further movement at Roy Shriver's trailer. Maybe he was asleep. I hoped so, because I intended to pay him a visit and it would be much better for him if he was, and if he remained that way. I carried my camera with me and made my way down the east-facing slope.

Brutus pushed himself up, tail wagging, and came over. I scratched his ears a while, never taking my eyes off Roy's trailer. I whispered for Brutus to lie down and be a good boy and, when he did, I moved quietly onto the sagging porch. I kept to the outside of the rotted planks where there was less chance of the wood squeaking. The screen door stood partly open, the main door behind it jammed firmly closed. I set the camera on the porch, up against the house, and put my ear to the door, listening, trying to ignore the heat that burned the side of my face.

I heard nothing except the incessant buzzing of a million flies.

The doorknob was hot. I turned it one degree every ten seconds. It took almost two minutes before I felt the door sag. I lifted the knob to take as much weight off the hinges as I could. When I got the door open a foot, I slipped inside and reversed the process, closing the door against the jamb without setting the latch.

It was almost dark inside. I was standing in a narrow hall. The first thing that assailed me was the smell. Human sweat, dried and musky, the sweat of dishonest labour. Years of it reeked through the floor, the walls and the ceiling. I breathed through my mouth, not wanting to smell any more of Roy Shriver than I had to.

But I sure could taste him.

I moved left down the hall into a filthy kitchen. Pots and pans and soiled plates lay stacked in a grubby sink. They spilled out onto the chipped draining board. The stove belonged in a war museum. The fridge door was grubby from a thousand filthy handprints, and the bare linoleum was cracked to oblivion. A handgun rested on top of the microwave. I moved in for a closer look. It was a Beretta and it looked well-oiled. If it were mine, I wouldn't keep it on the microwave.

I stood silently, breathing slowly, wondering if he wore his key to bed or if he hung it up some place.

I moved into the living room, the room closest to the barn. It was a mess of mismatched furniture: a sagging chesterfield that had once been orange; an old floor-model television. Another gun sat on top of the television, a Smith & Wesson this time. It looked to be the cleanest thing in the room. An array of TV tables were piled high with the remains of dinners past. I looked around the walls. No key. I moved back to the front door, then along the hall to the lion's den.

There were three doors ahead of me.

All were tightly closed.

The smell of the place made my nostrils ache. I thought I might sneeze. I tried to imagine the result of such a catastrophe.

Then I heard a noise.

A toilet flushed somewhere ahead of me.

Did he have an ensuite?

Or had he been in the main bathroom when I broke in? Were we about to come face-to-face?

I waited, ready for anything. I pressed an ear against the far door. I could hear something. Water running. The toilet. Then the sound of someone moving across the room. He'd finished in the bathroom. He was on the move.

Then I heard the sound of him falling into bed. He bounced once. Twice. Then lay still. I waited him out. Cleared my mind. Stood motionless outside Roy Shriver's bedroom door, almost without breathing. Minutes passed. Maybe even an hour. Then I heard snoring. Deep, rhythmic sounds that rattled the walls.

I let that part of myself that had been absent come back to Shriver's trailer; I let myself back into the moment.

Into the *now*.

It took five long minutes to open his door. The wave of heat, the stench of beer and human sweat and other smells I had no wish to identify, rolled out through the vertical opening as I lifted the doorknob and moved the door slowly and soundlessly over the threadbare carpet.

The room was a shambles. A dresser piled high with old clothes, a chair in the corner buried beneath a pile of hunting magazines, the bed against the far wall a riot of sweaty grey tangled sheets, and on the bedside table, in plain sight, another inevitable handgun, this one a 9 mm Glock. Roy Shriver was a man of infinite tastes in small arms. From where I stood, the Glock gleamed a dull gunmetal grey, confirming my earlier impression that he took better care of his handguns than any other damned thing he owned.

In the middle of the vile pile of bedding lay Roy Shriver, naked as the day he was born, flat on his back, his head thrust back, a pillow beneath his neck, both of which needed a good washing. His genitalia lay like a nest of sleeping gerbils and I was happy to let them sleep, though my baser instincts were to slice them off with the rusty hunting knife that hung on the far wall.

I looked behind the door, and lo and behold, there was a shotgun leaning against the door jamb, and I had no doubt it was fully loaded. It was double-barrelled, what they call an o/u, meaning the barrels were stacked vertically, not side-by-side. And someone had sawed both barrels down to about twelve inches and had fitted a folding stock. I saw a handful of twelve-gauge shells on the corner of the dresser. Buckshot, but this was a gun never intended for use against any four-legged prey. It was a close-quarters gun, designed to rip a hole through any two-legged animal foolish enough to come within twenty-five feet of the damned thing. I wondered if I could hide it, and was squatting next to it when Shriver made a sudden sound and jolted half upright.

I stayed low but I was clearly visible, head and shoulders above the level of his bed. He lay propped on an elbow and wiped the back of his free hand across his mouth. He hadn't noticed me at all. He blinked a few times, then rolled over onto his side, giving me the sort of knees-up view that would make a proctologist blush.

I stayed put for almost ten minutes, until my knees begged for mercy. I made a deal with them. I'd get up off them if they promised not to crack on the way.

I'd had quite enough crack for one day.

They kept their promise. I moved silently around Shriver's bed and into his bathroom. And there it was, curled in the sink like a rattlesnake. I reached out and hooked a finger through the dark, sweat-stained leather, careful not to clink the key against the porcelain. It swung free and I caught it cleanly in my other hand, backing out of his bedroom as carefully as I'd gone in.

I just hoped he wouldn't wake up for another pee before I had the chance to return the damned thing.

The thought of tiptoeing through his trailer again later did nothing to calm me as I lifted the front door closed. I retrieved my camera with Brutus watching me, a wary eye now, uncertain if I'd switched sides, coming, as I was, out of the enemy's trailer. I gave him a reassuring thumbs-up but he kept his distance.

The padlock was well oiled. It occurred to me to return the key there and then and to come back and explore the barn at my leisure, but I was working against time as I had no idea when Victor might be back.

It was a heavy door and it swung outwards as soon as I

popped the padlock from the chain. A wave of putrid heat hit me like a tsunami and I took a deep breath of outside air before stepping inside. I reached back and pulled the door closed behind me. There was a crude bar nailed to the left-hand door jamb. I dropped it into the metal latch welded to the inside of the door. It wouldn't hold back a determined ten-year-old for very long, but it was all there was.

Hanging beside the door was another sawed-off shotgun, a match for the one in Shriver's bedroom. It hung next to an ammo belt, ringed with twelve-gauge buckshot shells. With only one way in and out of the barn, it was probably the only defense they needed. I wondered if it had ever been used.

The barn had originally been built with eight stalls, four either side of a wide central corridor. It was a barn intended for horses. Big ones. Each stall measured at least fifteen feet across and eight feet deep. The doors had all been removed, and short wooden walls had been nailed across the openings. These wooden walls were three feet high and their purpose was abundantly clear. They held back the tons of topsoil that had been used to partially fill each stall. And in each stall, rows of healthy-looking marijuana plants flourished in the nutrient-rich soil. If I remember right, marijuana takes a month or two to mature before it blooms. The male plants are culled from the grow beds as soon as they are discovered, since they produce neither flowers nor buds, and if they are allowed to pollinate the females, the potency of the pot is pretty crappy.

It's a bit like marrying your sister.

Your kids will turn out to be the village idiots.

Above the plants, rows of fluorescent lights hung from adjustable chains in each stall. Judging from the smell, they'd used horse manure to nurture the weed. From where I stood, I'd say they had used tons of the stuff.

I could feel sweat rolling down my body. It was like moving through a rain forest. The high humidity made breathing difficult. I wouldn't want to stay too long inside this particular jungle. I'd seen a collection of face masks hanging near the door, all of them well-used and horribly grubby. I decided to take my chances breathing without one. I think the odds of catching a respiratory disease would be greatly increased by actually using one of the masks. I moved down the centre aisle and began taking photographs. I wasn't worried about the flash being seen from the outside because sheets of white-painted plywood had been hung all the way along the outside walls, covering every square inch of window space and forming a reflective surface for the fluorescent lights. Cowls of reflective metal hung above the lights, casting their sunshine glow back down amidst the lush, green foliage.

Two long wooden shelves, attached to the stalls, ran down both sides of the middle corridor. They'd placed milk jugs every foot or so along both shelves. I sniffed the open neck of several containers. They held a bubbling yeast solution that emitted carbon dioxide. When you're growing a lot of pot in a confined space, I guess you need extra carbon dioxide to help the plants grow faster. Most modern grow-ops use carbon dioxide machines, but, from what I was seeing, the Shrivers' grow-op was a little behind the times and wasn't likely to upset the balance of drug power anytime soon.

A dull throbbing, more a vibration in the air than an actual sound, came from the room at the far end of the barn and I guessed that's where I'd find the generator. Actually a pair of them, running hot with several five-gallon containers of gasoline standing on the floor nearby. There were two big extractor fans hooked to a maze of pipes that came in above the fluorescents like huge metal snakes. The exhaust fans sucked fresh air in from outside and sent the pot-rich air up through charcoal filters, putting the filtered air out into the atmosphere. City growers used ozone filters to neutralize the smell of the pot, but out here on the acreage, with no neighbours for at least half a mile, charcoal was probably just fine. I took more photos, moving down the centre lane and taking close-ups of the irrigation system. I shot photographs of the bags of fertilizer, high in potassium and nitrogen, lining the end wall of the generator room. It must have been a full-time job keeping the balance of nutrients just right in the irrigation system.

After ten minutes, I decided I'd had enough. I opened the door carefully, checked that the coast was clear and stepped out of the jungle. Every stitch of clothing was stuck to me. Sweat rolled down my brow, stinging my eyes. I locked the door and moved to the rear of the barn.

A large rusted white cylinder lay in a long metal rack. It was a propane tank, which explained how they were able to keep the barn super-heated without alerting the gas company. They simply purchased propane from various suppliers, none of whom were required to report their sales to the RCMP. The gas company that supplied natural gas to heat the trailers never saw a dramatic increase in product use, so there was never anything suspicious to report. Which is how the Shrivers' pot farm stayed under the radar.

I walked to the old man's trailer and stowed the camera on the edge of the deck. It took me just as long to return the padlock key as it had to locate it. I was aware that I probably stunk worse than the occupant by this time. I edged my way into his bedroom, thankful that he hadn't moved and that he was snoring loudly. I tiptoed to his bathroom and laid the key in the sink, letting the greasy leather string curl around the inside of the bowl like a long, thin snake.

The outside doorknob was even hotter but I held it tightly and lifted the trailer door closed behind me.

Christ!

I was glad that was over.

I had all the evidence I needed to show to Nicole Laurin at the Okotoks RCMP. Maybe she'd lock up Roy and Victor Shriver until after fight night.

Except it didn't work out that way.

Because when I turned to retrieve my camera, it was gone.

Chapter Twenty-Five

SHE WAS SQUATTING BESIDE the well between the trailers, her dress hanging down between her spread thighs. The well cover was open and she held a stick out over the hole.

My camera hung from the end of the stick.

"They drilled this well in nineteen eighty-six, when the old one ran dry," she said. "If I'm remembering right, it's a hundred and sixty-five feet deep."

"Ruby." I spoke softly. "I saw what he did to you. I imagine it wasn't the first time. But it could be the last. Come away with me. Bring the baby. I promise you, they'll never find you."

She stared at me for long seconds before speaking.

"Why are you here?"

"I'm still trying to stop the fight."

"With this?" She jiggled the stick, and the camera twitched as though it were alive.

"Yes."

She was a lot smarter than anyone gave her credit for.

But then I already knew that.

She looked from me to the barn, then back to me for a long, appraising moment. Then, without looking down, she let the end of the stick drop, and my camera fell into the open mouth of the well.

It fell one hundred and sixty-five feet, accelerating at thirty-two feet per second, squared. In less than three seconds, it smashed to pieces in a series of muted, metallic shrieks.

"You may leave now," she said, without getting up.

"Is this what you want? Is this the life you have chosen for you and your baby?"

"If you're still here when he wakes up, he'll kill you."

She stood up, brushed dust from the hem of her skirt and began to walk to her trailer.

"You didn't answer my question," I said, without raising my voice.

She slowed, turned to face me. She cocked her head and pulled her dress up high to reveal her panties.

"Did you," she said, "take enough pictures?"

I didn't know what to say. I had thought of them as evidence. Or that I could use them to blackmail the bastard into leaving her alone.

Touch her again and I'll show the photos to your son.

Something like that.

I knew my reasons were pure.

And yet, at the sight of her standing there like that, I felt nothing but cold shame and guilt.

She let the dress fall back and I knew I'd lost her. She'd been betrayed by every man she'd ever met.

"I'm sorry, Ruby."

She stared at me, the expression on her face unknowable.

Except, of course, I knew.

"As I said the first time, I don't like you." She waved me away like she would a small, annoying animal. "I still don't."

She turned and walked away, disappearing inside her trailer.

Chapter Twenty-Six

I STARED AT HER CLOSED TRAILER door, feeling soiled and experiencing emotions I really didn't like. I stood for long moments without moving.

Way, way too long.

As it turned out.

When I turned, Roy Shriver was waiting for me, standing hip-cocked and barefoot, the sawed-off shotgun centred squarely on my chest. At that range, the buckshot would turn me into uncooked hamburger meat.

He never said a word, just stood there like a gunfighter in some lawless frontier town facing down the local sheriff.

Except I wore no badge. No five-pointed silver star was pinned to my shirt. And no six-guns hung from leather holsters, guns that I could whip out and use to shoot the sawed-off from his hands.

"Oh, hi there," I said, but he didn't respond.

We stood like this for about ten seconds before he moved, turning his head towards Ruby's trailer.

"Ruby!" He bellowed, scaring a flock of sparrows from

a nearby tree.

I didn't look back when her trailer door came open. I sensed rather than saw her, standing in direct sunlight on the bleached wooden porch.

"Who the fuck is this?" Shriver asked,

The shotgun never wavered.

I heard her step down off the deck and could tell from the way Shriver watched her that she was coming up close to my left side.

Shriver moved the shotgun like a pointing stick.

"Move," he said to her.

When she walked past me, she was well outside my reach. He probably figured I'd grab her, use her as a shield. Which was the last thing on my mind. She walked up to her father-in-law and handed him something.

"What's that?" He scowled at her.

She never wavered, just kept her arm extended, holding a small piece of paper. I could see he was pissed off, but he reached out and snatched the paper from her outstretched hand.

It was my business card.

He read it.

"What the fuck are you doing here?" he asked me.

I shrugged.

"Where'd you get this?" He waved my card in Ruby's face, and I thought he was going to smack her.

So did Ruby, and she flinched, raising a protective arm to ward off a potential blow. Which made me wonder who it was who kept putting Ruby in the hospital.

"I gave it to her," I said. "Just now." He stared at me. "A

few minutes ago. I'm looking for Victor Shriver."

"Shut. The. Fuck. Up." He turned back to Ruby. "I asked you a question, girl."

"He gave it to me. He said he's looking for Vic."

Roy Shriver's eyes narrowed, his face pinched in. He clearly didn't believe what he was being told here.

"What's he want with Vic?"

She shrugged.

"Don't lie to me, girl."

"I'm trying to stop a fight," I said.

Without a moment's hesitation, Roy Shriver turned and fired the first barrel of the shotgun at me. He lowered the barrel, like the police in the southern States had learned to do, maximizing the ricochet effect of the buckshot. When the cops do it, they fire down into asphalt or concrete, so the shot bounces off and spreads out, giving it a wider scatter pattern while depleting its velocity.

So you broaden your influence but lessen your impact.

But it still hurts like hell.

In Shriver's case, he fired into a mixture of dirt and rock, stones and gravel. The shot pattern was wildly erratic with balls of lead flying off in all directions.

But not that erratic because three pellets hit me, two in the left leg and one in the shoulder.

Imagine being stung by the world's nastiest bumblebee.

Times three.

You're not even close.

It hurt like hell. The shot to the shoulder bounced off bone and pushed me back a full step. The two in my left leg buckled me, and I fell on my side. Blood flowed from two

holes in my left thigh. When I got to my feet, I felt it running down into my shoe.

"Tol' you to shut the fuck up, Mr. Private Eye."

I nodded.

I'd acquiesce.

For now.

He turned to Ruby, lifted his chin for her to continue.

She looked shaken but it was nothing she hadn't seen
before, I was certain of that.

"He said he wanted to talk to Vic about that boxing
match. Said he'd been hired to stop it."

"Who by?"

"The other guy's wife," she said.

"And?"

"I told him Vic wasn't here. I told him to leave."

She stood with her head bowed, looking at the ground.
Shriver considered her a moment, then turned his attention to me.

"She tell you to leave?"

"Yessir."

"Git over here," he said.

I wasn't sure how much weight my leg would take. I
managed a sort of hopping gait but I was pretty sure I could
put more weight on it than that. When I was maybe fifteen
feet from him, well within killing range of the other barrel,
he motioned me to stop.

"She tell it right?" He raised his chin an inch.

"Yes. Paul Miller's wife is terrified. She thinks her husband could get seriously hurt. Thinks he might even get
killed in the ring."

"She hired you?"

"She did."

"What's it worth?"

He was a quick study.

"What will it take?"

"What you offering?"

"I'm not authorized to talk numbers, Mr. Shriver. Just to sound Victor out."

"Never mind Vic," he said. "You talk t'anyone, you talk to me."

"Understood."

"They got money?"

"Some. Not a lot."

He stared at my card.

"This your number?"

I nodded. Blood from my running shoe was pooling on the ground.

"Now git."

I started towards the drive, and after twenty yards, Shriver called after me.

"You going to hospital with that?"

I shook my head.

"You better not!"

We both understood that if I went to hospital with a gunshot wound, the hospital would have to report it to the cops.

And Roy Shriver wanted no truck with the cops.

"If you change your mind —" he levelled the shotgun directly at my head. "Fuck the ricochet. Next one takes your head off."

There was not much to say to that. As I turned to leave, I heard the sound of a motor, saw the dust cloud trailing it up the drive.

It was Victor.

Home with his spoils.

He almost drove past me, but then he hit the brakes and skidded the car through ninety degrees. He jumped out before the car had even stopped moving.

"What the fuck are you doin' here?" he screamed at me. He saw his father holding the shotgun, saw the blood running down my leg, staining my pants. "You shoot him, Daddy?"

"What's it to you?" Roy said.

"That's the son of a bitch sucker-punched me at Steve's!"

"You don't say."

Victor stormed towards his father.

"Gimme the fuckin' gun!" he yelled.

I kept walking down the drive. Limping, really. If he were going to shoot me, he'd shoot me in the back just as soon as shoot me in the chest. I heard Roy speak, and Victor yelled again. Then a hard sound, like a slap.

I didn't hear anything after that.

Didn't need to.

I could guess what had happened. Son loses his temper, father slaps son across the face, end of story.

I continued walking down the long drive. I'd return for my belongings in the narrow gully some other time.

But I wouldn't be coming back empty-handed.

Chapter Twenty-Seven

I SAT ON A TREE STUMP a mile west of the Shriver acreage, my leg throbbing like a drum skin and my shoulder as sore as hell. I mourned the loss of my seventeen-hundred-dollar Canon Sure Shot. Not that I blamed Ruby. It was my fault. I felt sick to my stomach from guilt and from the sense of screwing up on the job. It was not a nice feeling.

In the distance, the blacktop rose to meet the blue horizon before it disappeared over a short rise. In the heat shimmer, a scene from every other Hollywood movie played out as a yellow Mustang convertible came burbling over the rise. A V8 GT convertible, all three hundred horses running wild. I guessed it was Danny. One never knew what make, model or colour of car he might be driving on any given day.

I was right.

He pulled over, then made a tire-squealingly tight one-eighty and pulled up next to me at the side of the road. He pushed his sunglasses up onto his forehead with the first finger of his right hand.

"Ola," he said. "You look like sheeeet."

"Really? I feel like a million bucks."

I looked into the open car. The interior was black leather.

"I'm likely to bleed on your upholstery," I said.

"Not my upholstery," he said. He looked at my leg and took in the torn shirt and damage to my shoulder. "You need ze hospital, hombre?"

"Yeah," I answered. "But I'm not going. I called Cindy. She'll take care of it."

I'd remembered to take my cell phone off vibrate and put it on the ringer. I climbed into the Mustang smelling worse than a dead skunk.

"Phew! You wanna ride in the trunk, padre?"

I considered it for a moment.

"How 'bout I drive and you ride in the trunk?" I suggested.

"Fine by me. Long as I don't need to sit next to you, el stinko."

"I've smelled worse," I said.

"Uh-huh." He shook his head.

"So hold your nose, Tonto."

I buckled up, and he slid his sunglasses onto the bridge of his nose. The Mustang was a stick shift. He snuck it into first and hit the gas.

You can't drive the Mustang GT at anything like sensible speeds. The speedometer was well into three figures within a matter of seconds. I thought the back end wanted to overtake us. We took the little rise at one-sixty and I swear we were airborne for several seconds before he backed off and let friction overtake the force of gravity on the downhill run.

"I'm guessing things did not go well, amigo," he said.

"You always were the observant one," I said. "And you're right. They didn't."

"Open the glove box."

I popped open the glove box. Inside lay a brushed chrome Thermos flask. I unscrewed the lid and poured myself a steaming coffee. My first in three long days. I sank into the leather upholstery and sipped it, feeling it lift my spirits as only a good cup of fresh java can.

"So." He downshifted and pulled out past a truck towing a trailer. When he pulled back over, he said, "I'm all ears."

"I don't think you want to hear this," I said.

"You're not your brother's keeper, Eddie. Stop trying to protect me. I'm guessing it has something that will remind me of Cathy."

Damn.

"Am I right?"

"I'm supposed to be the detective," I said.

He looked at me.

"You are. And a damned good one. I appreciate what you're trying to do but it was a long time ago and you can't protect me for the rest of my life. Or yours."

I watched the scenery slide past the window.

"Okay," I said. "But stop me if any of this gets too much."

"You have my word."

"Fair enough."

"And tell me everything. Leave no stone unturned."

So I began at the beginning.

And, as requested, I turned every stone.

Chapter Twenty-Eight

CATHY MANY-GUNS WAS Danny's younger sister. She was twenty-five the day I met her. And she was Hollywood's dream of a North American Indian Princess. She had Danny's build, lithe and athletic, but not his height. She had high cheekbones and full lips, glossy black hair that appeared blue in almost any light, and soft brown eyes. She had a stillness about her that defied description. Like Danny, she could stand and absorb her surroundings without disturbing them.

Yet she did disturb.

Especially men.

Especially me.

This was years before I met Cindy Palmer.

Cathy Many-Guns announced her engagement on her twenty-fifth birthday, to a man named Kevin LaFournier. He claimed native blood on his grandfather's side, but seemed vague beyond that. Cathy clearly loved him. I stood on the sidelines and watched as she broke my heart and married him the following summer. They lived on the reserve west of

Calgary, in a three-bedroom, rancher-style bungalow with a barn and corrals where Cathy rode her three horses every day.

Jealousy aside, there was something about LaFournier that disturbed me. He had a wild side, a dark streak that I sensed far more than I saw. Slowly, as the weeks turned to months, Cathy began to withdraw — nothing much at first, just saying she wanted to spend more time at the house. She began excusing herself from family gatherings, saying they were busy, that Kevin wasn't feeling well or that one of her horses was sick.

They missed a complete Christmas, and by spring, Danny admitted to being worried. Kevin had bought a dog, a big, shaggy thing that looked half-wolf, and it scared most of the family from visiting Cathy's home. By summer, Cathy was all but a memory. No one had seen or heard from her in months. I suspected that Kevin LaFournier was cutting her off, limiting her access to the outside world for his own selfish reasons. He'd had the home phone line disconnected months before, and Cathy hadn't answered Danny's mail all year. When he stopped by, she seemed vague and distant. Gone was the funny, friendly Cathy of old. Now, even Danny felt like an intruder.

It was late in the afternoon, a Sunday, when we paid a surprise visit. It had been Cathy's birthday the week before, and Danny had bought her a puppy. A golden Lab. A shy little thing that needed to be nurtured, to be loved. Danny wanted to know if she was still enjoying the puppy. He picked me up from my house, saying very little all the way out to his sister's place. The yard was rundown, the veranda littered with beer cans. The whole place looked to be in disrepair.

"Can you believe this?" Danny asked.

I shook my head.

I had a bad feeling, too.

We knocked, and when nobody answered, we tried the door. It was not locked. I followed Danny in. The inside was even worse than we were expecting. Lamps broken, end tables turned over, books and magazines strewn across the floor.

We found Kevin passed out, fully clothed, lying across the bed in the master bedroom, his muddy boots marking up the bedspread. He snored loudly and he reeked of beer. I stared down at him. He'd put on weight, ballooning over the past year, his belly massive, his neck thick with double chins.

"He likes the beer, eh?" Danny nodded at him.

"You've got that right."

Cathy was downstairs, the puppy curled in her lap. She'd been crying, and her face was a mess. She had a bruise under her right eye, her lip was swollen, and she was missing an inch of scalp.

Her beautiful hair.

She refused to blame her husband. It was her fault, she said. She pushed all the wrong buttons and got what she deserved. Danny pleaded with her to come away with us. She refused. She was a strong woman. A woman who took her wedding vows very seriously. She would not leave her husband.

Nor would she blame him.

I was with Danny a month later when he got the call from someone on the Band Council. Nobody knew where

Cathy was. They hadn't been able to reach her. Nor Kevin. They were worried about Cathy's horses. They'd been acting strangely for two days.

We took every corner on two wheels, or so it seemed, and to hell with the posted limit. The drive up to Cathy's bungalow was covered in snow, and Danny spun the truck a one-eighty and was out the door before me. A pair of horse trailers stood in the drive. Snow had drifted along the exposed side of the old one, which had a broken axle. It was parked tight against the fence, long past any semblance of usefulness. The other was hitched to a black truck, parked facing the house.

We ran across the open yard, in a hurry to escape the cold.

The wind was something else. It came in hard off the mountains and blew in strong, powerful gusts, dropping the air temperature below the posted minus twenty-five. At night, it dropped even lower. Last night, it had hit minus thirty-five, without the wind-chill factor. Not a record, but bitterly cold nonetheless. We could hear the horses, whinnying for feed and for fresh water, around the back of the house.

We didn't bother knocking, just hit the front door hard and ran inside.

I wished I hadn't.

"Jee-sus! What's that smell?"

I covered my mouth and nose, breathing in air filtered through my winter gloves.

"Cathy!" Danny called for his sister. He listened but there was no reply.

We moved quickly through the house, searching every room. The main floor gave up nothing. As we moved down the stairs to the basement, the awful smell got worse. I felt like gagging. We searched each room in the basement. There was a spare bedroom, empty and unused, and Cathy's sewing room. Before her marriage she had been a seamstress, taking in small jobs to help out her family. But she'd given it up almost a year ago.

We didn't find Kevin until we got to the L-shaped family room at the far end of the basement. He was waiting for us, naked, sitting upright in the Boston rocker.

"Jesus H. Christ," Danny whispered. "What the hell has been going on down here?"

I could barely speak. The overhead light was just a naked twenty-five-watt bulb. It threw a dim glow over the far end of the room. Beneath it, Kevin sat like some godawful bloated nightmare creature, barely recognizable as a human being anymore.

He was lashed upright to the big rocking chair. His clothes had been cut or torn from his body. His arms and legs had been duct-taped to the chair. The duct tape ran in circles up both forearms and around his shins all the way down to his ankles. It was extraordinarily neat. Whoever did it had no intention of him escaping.

Ever.

His entire body was covered in welts. Red lumps. Oozing sores. They were everywhere. Red and angry. I couldn't make out what the hell they were. Like bee stings. But bigger. Much bigger. And they seemed to pulse, to throb quietly, each with a life all its own. I had no clue what was wrong with him.

The plague?

I was almost prepared to believe that. Except this had been done on purpose. It had been inflicted. The plague belongs to Mother Nature. And, bad as she might be, Mother Nature's never this cruel.

Danny moved closer.

"Is he still alive?" I asked.

Then I saw his chest move up a quarter inch. A shuddery movement, before it dropped back down. Danny looked at me.

"I think so," he said.

We should have called nine-one-one.

But we hadn't found Cathy yet.

The family room was part kitchen, and the Boston rocker sat on the lino in the makeshift kitchen portion. It contained a small stove, a bar fridge and a fold-down table.

I moved on.

And found the puppy next.

The blood on the wall led me to him. He lay discarded like an old rag doll. More dead than alive, lying in the corner, broken bones showing through his bloodied fur. I took his snout, stroked it softly, almost wept when he licked my hand. It didn't take a detective to figure out what had happened. Someone had held him by the back legs and had slammed him against the wall.

More than once.

The blood splatter told the story.

I pulled out my cell phone. I called the vet, someone I knew. I told him to hurry. Told him I'd pay any speeding fines, just get here.

Now.

I went quickly back to the kitchen.

"She isn't in the house," I told Danny.

He seemed fascinated by the thing that had been Kevin LaFournier. I couldn't think of this thing as a part of the human race anymore. As I watched, Danny reached out, touched Kevin on the cheek. Kevin flinched, sucked air in like a drowning man.

His eyelids flew open.

I almost threw up.

His eyes were full of metal.

Danny steeled himself and touched him again.

"Can you hear me? Kevin? Can you hear me?"

Kevin made a noise, something from deep inside the folds of his throat.

"Where's Cathy? Where is my sister?"

He said something, but it was impossible to understand him. He grew frantic, straining against the tape that bound him to the chair. His face grew red.

Redder.

He heaved against the duct tape, his whole body rigid with pain. I watched in fascinated horror as some of the red sores on his face burst open, and a thick yellow pus seeped out.

His entire body was riddled with infection.

But it was the thing in the centre of the pus that was hard to comprehend.

"Danny?"

He turned to me. I pointed to whatever it was protruding from a sore on Kevin's face.

"Is that what I think it is?"

He looked at it. Then he stepped around Kevin and picked up a saucepan from the stove. He lifted the lid and stared at the contents.

"What is that?" I asked him.

He didn't answer, just held it out at arm's length. I peered inside. The bottom of the saucepan was thick with congealed feces. It smelled like dog poo. Someone had boiled it. And had tipped in a full box of sewing pins. Hundreds upon hundreds of them.

"What the hell happened to him?" I asked.

Danny reached out, took the head of a pin protruding from Kevin's cheek and slowly withdrew it. Kevin sucked air between his teeth. Close up, I could see the heads of more.

Buried in Kevin's flesh.

In his eyes.

Dozens. Hundreds. Maybe even thousands.

There wasn't a square inch of his body left unattended. His groin was a swollen, angry mass. I tried to imagine how it must have felt, having hundreds of pins pushed deep inside my penis and testicles.

I couldn't.

Be thankful for small mercies.

"She did this." Danny's voice was flat, matter-of-fact.

I'd pretty much reached the same conclusion. The new puppy, not housebroken, had angered him. Maybe the puppy had pooped on the carpet. Kevin had punished him, thrashing him into the wall until he was almost dead.

And then what?

More beer. Until he passed out. The rest is history. She duct tapes him to the rocker. Cuts off all his clothes. Then boils up the puppy's feces. With the sewing pins.

I wondered how many pins she had stuck in him before he awoke.

Not many.

He must have screamed. He must have threatened her, then cajoled her, then begged her to stop. But by then, she was past the point of no return. She was reliving every beating, every miserable thing he'd ever done to her. It was the passion of revenge that kept her going.

But going where?

We had to find her.

Time was running out.

And fast.

We went upstairs and opened the front door, intending to search outside, not expecting what was waiting for us out there. Kevin's half-wolf dog was blocking the exit.

"Don't move," Danny said softly. "Don't look him in the eye."

I already knew that much. But couldn't take my damned eyes off him. He was huge, his fangs an ugly yellow beneath his curled upper lip.

"Lick your lips," Danny said.

"What?"

"Lick your lips."

I did as he told me. The wolf-dog uncurled its lip.

"Again."

I licked them like there was no tomorrow.

As indeed there may not have been.

We waited for long minutes. My lips were getting sore, the icy wind cracking them as I continued to lick. He told me later that it's a pack thing. The alpha male doesn't like to be challenged. Licking your lips is a sign of submission. A sign that you've conceded defeat. He's unlikely to attack you once he knows you've submitted to him. Finally, the wolf-dog turned and jumped down from the porch. We watched him until he was out of sight.

"Jesus." I let out the breath I'd been holding since I'd first stepped out on the porch.

"He won't be back," Danny said, and I hoped he was right.

We split up. Danny went to search the corrals and the horse shelters. I stayed closer to the house. I searched the truck and the newer horse trailer, but both were empty. The keys were hanging in the truck's ignition. That didn't tell me anything. People in the country leave their keys in their cars all the time. They rarely lock up their houses.

I stood in the wind, looking round the yard. There was a thin, worn path running from the back of the old discarded trailer down to the gate in the corral.

Why would anyone even keep an old, discarded trailer? Despite the wind, there were still traces of hay twigs trodden into the narrow pathway. Something blowing in the wind caught my eye.

A broken piece of twine.

And suddenly, I understood what had happened.

Sometimes it doesn't pay to be a detective.

"Danny!"

He came at a run from the far side of the corral, all three of Cathy's horses running behind him. I waited until he got close before I stopped him.

"Wait here," I said.

He moved forward two steps, but I held my arm out.

"No. Let me do this."

There was only one door on the old trailer. It opened across the back, and the outside latch was in the closed position. When I lifted it, the steel handle sent a cold shock through my hand.

The door swung open with a loud creak. The piece of broken twine hung from the top of the trailer, too short to hold the door. I found a piece of broken branch and wedged the door open.

I stepped inside.

She was waiting for me at the far end.

Cathy had been using the old trailer to store hay for the horses. She was on her last bale. She'd sliced it open and had carried several armfuls out to feed her horses while Kevin sat naked in the basement, his body compromised by steel pins. She'd gone back for the last armful of hay, climbed into the old trailer, and the twine holding the door open had snapped when the heavy door, hanging at a crazy angle because of the missing wheel, had finally worn it out. The door had no inside latch. It had slammed shut, locking her inside.

Kevin was already feeling the effects of an infection that would soon run rampant through his bloodstream. An infection that he would endure without relief for the next forty-eight hours.

It was a wonder he wasn't dead.

Not that I cared. The son of a bitch didn't deserve to live. But Cathy was already gone.

I took off my coat and laid it round her shoulders. A useless gesture. Her body was frozen solid, her arms locked tight around her chest, her face a tableau of total despair. I tried to close her eyes but the lids wouldn't move. I was afraid they might snap if I kept trying. I sat with her on her bit of hay. She was curled in the far corner, huddled tight for the last vestige of warmth she could muster.

I hoped she had passed quickly, had died in peace, but I knew that was near impossible.

Danny was standing where I'd left him.

He knew, of course.

Of course he knew.

I put my arms around him. It was like hugging a tree. He remained unbending until the cold made me shiver. He took off his coat and gave it to me. I watched him climb into the horse trailer.

He never made a sound.

That was almost eight years ago.

The vet had arrived and given the puppy a shot. He tried hard not to look down the far end of the basement, where paramedics were silently cutting duct tape from Kevin LaFournier's arms and legs.

Kevin lasted thirty-six hours at the Foothills Hospital, almost an hour's drive away. The attending doctors told me later there wasn't enough narcotic medication on hand to rid him of his pain. They made him as comfortable as they could by putting him in a deep coma. The police were furious, demanding they be allowed to interview him. They tried to get me to reconstruct what had happened, but I remained as mute as LaFournier. As mute as Cathy.

The family had a quiet and very private funeral for her. Even I wasn't invited. And after that, Danny simply went away. Disappeared. He was gone for more than a year. No messages, no notes, no email. Nothing.

And then, on Christmas Eve, he arrived on my doorstep with a gift for me. He didn't stay, merely smiled, handed me a beautifully wrapped, priceless Indian artifact and promised not to be a stranger.

We've never spoken of Cathy or Kevin LaFournier since.

The vet was able to save Cathy's puppy, though it still walks with an odd, hind-leg limp. Danny arranged for someone in his family to care for the dog. I received a call from one of Danny's many cousins a month after Danny disappeared, asking me if I could take the puppy.

I was tempted but realized it wouldn't be fair on the dog. I don't have the sort of lifestyle that favours pets. Not pets who require someone to love them twenty-four hours a day. They found someone else. Not a problem, they said.

And so, now, whenever I take on a case that leans towards spousal abuse, I make of point of leaving Danny in the dark.

It's just better that way.

Chapter Twenty-Nine

WE PULLED UP ACROSS FROM Cindy Palmer's townhouse, in the visitor's parking lot. Danny shut off the motor and turned to face me.

"That was eight years ago," he said.

I nodded.

"Life goes on," he said. "At moments like this, I ask myself a question."

I waited.

"What would Cathy want me to do?"

"Good question."

"She said to tell you to move over."

"Move over?"

"As in, make room for me."

"You're sure?"

"Someone has to let Mr. Shriver know that payback is expensive."

I didn't ask him which particular Mr. Shriver he had in mind. I don't think it really mattered.

Cindy was expecting us, but even so, she was a little

upset. I may have minimalized it over the phone.

"You've been *shot!*" she said. Loudly.

"It appears so," I said. "There was a loud bang and my leg started bleeding."

"Just the one bang?"

"Just the one."

"But two holes?"

"Are you familiar with the workings of the sawed-off shotgun?" I said. "And the finer points of twelve-gauge buckshot? Ouch."

She'd stuck something into one of the holes in my leg.

"Nobody," she said, "likes a smartass. Off with the strides, Mr. Funnymouth."

I took my trousers off.

Carefully.

They laid me on a sheet of heavy plastic draped over the spare bed. A tray of surgical-looking instruments stood on the night table. I tried not to look at them, or think about how she had smuggled them out of the Rocky View.

"No needles, okay?" I reminded her of our agreement.

"Baby," she said. "As in —" and here she added air quotes "— crybaby."

I lay on the plastic in my underwear. Danny peered at the two pellet wounds in my left thigh.

"Do you know how deep they are?" he asked her.

"No," she said. "That's what these are for."

She held up a pair of long, thin tweezer-looking things, and I felt faint.

"Please don't do that," I pleaded.

Danny looked at me.

"Ah. Baby."

Smartass.

He handed me a piece of leather, thick as a Quarter Pounder. I got it in tight against my back teeth and bit down on it, just like they do in the duster movies, when the dishevelled-looking doc pulls a slug out of the hero's chest before sluicing it with a bottle of rotgut whiskey.

I took the leather out for a moment.

"Got any whiskey, Miss Kitty?"

Cindy smiled at me.

"With Coke, or straight up?"

"Straight up," I said.

"You might like something a little stronger by the time we're done here," she said. She put on her game face. "I'm going in."

She found the first pellet in about half a minute. It took a little longer than that to get it out, and it hurt a lot more than it did going in. Danny washed the wound with something that felt just like rotgut whiskey, and I might have called him a rude word or three. Then Cindy put two neat stitches through the hole and stuck a see-through plastic dressing over the wound.

"One down, one to go," she said. "Need a minute?"

I nodded.

Danny sat on the bed and doctored the wound in my shoulder.

"You were lucky," he said. "It ricocheted off the bone here."

When he touched it, to emphasize the word *here,* I almost bit his finger off.

"What part of 'lucky' am I not getting?" I asked him.

"It could have gone in under the skin and lodged behind the bone." He turned to Cindy. "Doubt even Miss Kitty here could get one of those out."

"Be fun trying, though," she said. "You ready, Hopalong?"

I bit down on the Quarter Pounder and nodded.

"Muffulunger."

Which was Early American parlance for *Holy crap, that hurt.*

~

Later, when the painkillers kicked in and the throbbing died down a few points, I made plans with Danny to take him to Bert's gym in a couple of days. Danny had agreed to teach Paul a few things that Bert couldn't, or shouldn't, since they definitely fell outside both the direction and spirit of the Queensberry Rules. Cindy cooked us supper and she thanked Danny for bringing me back to her in one piece.

Well. Sort of.

They hugged, and Danny lifted her off her feet.

Only because I couldn't.

Not without popping a few stitches.

Cindy had asked her ex-husband to take Lindsay for the night so I could stay over.

And stay horizontal.

After she'd cleaned up the kitchen, Cindy came and stood beside me as I stretched out on the couch beneath a comforter.

"How you holding up?" she asked.

"I'm great," I said.

"Need anything?"

I thought about it. The painkillers were working just fine.

"Nope," I said. "Unless you want to get naked and join me under the covers."

She grinned.

"Why waste a good horizontal?" she said, shucking off her scrubs.

I threw back the comforter.

"Or a good vertical."

Chapter Thirty

I SLIPPED AWAY FROM Cindy's townhouse bright and early the following morning. She had the next two days off and had agreed I could borrow her car for the morning. She drove a little red Saturn stick shift that cornered nicely and thrummed up the gearbox as fast as I could move the stick.

It was a little past dawn when I arrived at the Shriver place. I parked the Saturn facing towards the highway, should I need a fast getaway, and hobbled up their drive. Before I came in sight of the trailers, I stepped into the tall grass.

A westerly wind stirred the air, and I caught the scent of woodsmoke. It's a beautiful smell. It reminds everyone in Canada of time spent camping in the great outdoors. Visions of flat, crystal-clear lakes, of towering pines and endless blue skies filled my field of dreams. I was back hiking trails in the mountains, then on a beach in Ontario with my parents. Woodsmoke will do that to you. It's one of the most powerful aromas on the planet.

I reached the eastern slope and moved along its edge until I came to the gully. My belongings were just as I'd left them. I peered over the crest of the small hill.

I saw the origin of the woodsmoke.

The barn had gone.

In its place, a long, deep scar lay against the earth. Heavy timbers smoldered in the narrow pit. The devastation was total. Nothing was left standing. Had they harvested the pot? Or had they simply brought in a backhoe and set about destroying all evidence of their grow-op? I could see backhoe tracks everywhere. Whoever they'd hired had done a thorough job. Fresh dirt filled the hole, and I guessed the heavy timbers were the roof trusses, burning down to charcoal.

I looked for Brutus. He wasn't in the yard. But of course, they'd moved him. Or else the backhoe driver might have run him over.

So there went my last chance to secretly stop the fight. To force the Shrivers into forfeit. With my camera at the bottom of the well and the grow-op burned to the ground, I had nothing to take to the RCMP.

The Shrivers were free of the long arm of the law.

I looked at Roy Shriver's trailer. I was armed, of course. Danny had seen to that. But I wished I had a high-powered rifle instead of the little 9 mm that was digging into the small of my back. What I couldn't do to that trailer with a box of high-powered ammunition from my vantage point up on the gully. I'd blow the place to kingdom come. Roy Shriver and his gun collection along with it.

The morning sun came up over the eastern rim, warming everything on the eighty acres.

Almost everything.

In me, the blood ran cold.

192

Chapter Thirty-One

I MET DANNY AT BERT'S gym the following morning. Paul Miller was already out running wind sprints around the block and Valerie was with him.

"Bloody woman," Bert cursed her. "She quits smoking and has been bagging on me to quit ever since." He fired up a fresh smoke from the butt of his last one. "I told her, 'Get off my back, bitch, it ain't gonna happen.'"

"You called her a bitch, did you?" Danny asked.

"You met her?"

"Briefly."

"Would you call her a bitch?"

"Not to her face."

Bert smiled.

"Me, neither."

"How's Paul doing?" I asked.

"For his age? Okay, I guess."

"Does he stand a chance?"

"Of winning?" He sounded incredulous.

"No, Bert," I said. "Of going three rounds without

getting himself killed."

"Not a snowball's," he said. "Doubt he'll even go Round One."

Which wasn't what I wanted to hear.

"Does he know?" Danny asked.

"Christ, no," Bert said, coughing up a lung. "I need him confident. Tell him that, he's likely to worry about it, get clobbered as soon as he steps in the ring."

Danny looked at me. He didn't need to say anything.

"It'd help if young Danny here took him under his wing for a spell," Bert said.

"My pleasure," Danny said.

Bert smiled around his cigarette. "Then maybe he'll make it to Round Two," he said.

When Paul and Val came back, I introduced them to Danny, explaining that he was going to work with Paul in a more specialized capacity.

"Meaning what?" Val asked. "And why are you limping?"

"I've got a charley horse," I said.

She was watching Danny. When Danny moved into the ring with Paul, Val turned back to me.

"Who is that?" she asked.

"Danny Many-Guns."

"I know. But *who* is he?"

"He's a friend of mine."

"Really?" She watched Danny loosening up. "Is he married?"

"No. But you are."

She almost blushed.

"That obvious?"

"Uh-huh."

"Well, who can blame me? I mean, he's gorgeous."

"Indeed, he is."

She looked at the ring. Danny had stripped to the waist and he was already showing Paul a few moves. He had tribal scars across his pecs.

"He's very . . ." She looked at me. "What's the word I'm looking for?"

"Yummy."

She laughed.

"That wasn't it but it's close enough." She watched them some more. "Is it true boxers aren't supposed to have sex while they're training for a fight?"

"Apparently, that's true," I said.

"Don't tell Paul. I won't be taking no for an answer tonight."

She walked off, moving like a panther.

Or was that a cougar?

~

Danny worked with Paul for an hour. He showed him stuff boxers aren't supposed to know. He strapped pads on over his liver and taught Paul the Mexican hook, otherwise known as the rip. I saw Danny grimace a couple of times, so I knew that Paul's punching power had picked up.

Danny taught him to butt heads in a clinch, and how to avoid being butted. Most boxers who use the head butt make it look like an accident, not that the referee is ever really fooled, but by then, the damage is done. The skin over the eyes is prone to tearing, so a nasty butt can open up soft tissue early and make it bleed. The last thing you want is blood in your eyes. Once you've been cut open, your opponent will work it, continually hitting the same spot to force the cut wide open.

Another close-up nasty is the thumb gouge. As boxers tire, they tend to fall in on one another. When your head's resting on your opponent's shoulder, if the ref's not looking, your opponent might dig his thumb into your unprotected eye. Danny taught Paul how to avoid being gouged, and how to gouge back if the situation required it.

He showed Paul a bunch of other nasty tricks that are seriously frowned upon in the ring. We weren't suggesting that Paul employ any of them, but the fact was, he was up against a street fighter who had more dirty tricks up his sleeve than Paul ever would. We were merely evening up the odds. If Shriver tried anything underhanded, he might be surprised when Paul came back with a little something of his own.

Danny finished the session with something to tire any opponent. He showed Paul exactly where his opponent's heart lay, and then told him to pummel the area repeatedly.

"Do that hard and fast, fifteen or twenty times when you get him up against the ropes, or whenever you get the chance," Danny explained. "Short, hard jabs, straight over the heart. It's very tiring for you," he added. "But as much as it takes out of you, it goes double, or even triple, for him. It will wear him out real fast. It throws off the natural rhythms of his heartbeat."

"You mean, it might kill him?"

Danny shrugged.

"Do it long and hard enough, sure," he said. "But you don't have the power or the stamina to kill him. You do have the power to slow him down, and you have the strength to hurt him, maybe even put him down. I felt it in you. That right hook rocks."

"How about knocking him out?"

"One day at a time, little Grasshopper."

Danny bowed to Paul, then ducked between the ropes and went over to the speed bag to burn off the excess energy he'd been carrying all morning. He started slow but soon built up a rhythm that had almost everyone in the gym watching him. He played the bag, thrumming the back of his taped knuckles against the leather, building up to a blurring speed that made it appear as if he was punching a bag *inside* a bag. He kept it up for almost ten minutes, alternating the angle of attack as he worked from the waist up, keeping his legs moving. He finished with a sudden flurry that defied the laws of gravity and motion. Long after he'd finished, the gym echoed with the sound of the speed bag reverberating under the onslaught.

Everyone who'd been watching him suddenly found something to do when he stopped and walked away. He came over and offered to spar with me but I declined. My leg was much better but my shoulder still ached.

"Maybe tomorrow," I said.

We touched knuckles and he left without another word. Afterwards, the noise level in the gym got much louder as people began talking about him. He had that effect wherever he went.

I'm not sure if he knew that about himself.

Chapter Thirty-Two

WE WERE DOWN TO THE last week when it broke on the Internet. Someone had written something about it in their daily blog, and someone else had picked it up. There is nothing on earth that can match the speed of the Internet to make a person famous.

Or infamous.

Within half a day, the blogger's web page had crashed four times. By mid-afternoon, they'd recorded more than a hundred thousand hits. By midnight, ten times that number had logged on to read about "The Fight of the Century."

The Millers' phone had begun to ring long before that. Friends. Neighbours. Friends of friends. Friends of neighbours. "Is it true?" "Are you crazy?" "Are you in training?" "Can you get us tickets?"

Then, early the next morning, the local paper called, and the radio station. By lunchtime, seven major media outlets in Calgary had called, all wanting to set up exclusive interviews with Paul Miller. Without his permission, they were already running his picture on the evening news.

Someone had awakened a sleeping giant.

And it wasn't about to go back to sleep.

When Paul and Valerie awoke the following morning, their street was blocked by vans bristling with rooftop antennas, and parabolic tracking dishes that beamed fuzzy pictures of their living room to satellites circling the globe. Satellites that then sent those fuzzy pictures into a hundred million homes in every corner of the globe.

Suddenly, in just twenty-four hours, the story of Paul Miller's attempt to right a wrong had become the hottest thing in world news. CNN came. The FOX network. NBC, ABC, the BBC, Reuters, they all tuned in. Pay Per View negotiated the rights to broadcast the fight.

Live!

A change of venue was discussed. Someone suggested flying everyone down to Vegas. For the week. All expenses paid. We'll charter two jets. You can bring whomever you want. Two hotels had already confirmed, on camera, they would cover the family's room and board for the entire duration.

Win or lose, it was a win-win situation.

In a world gone suddenly mad, Paul Miller tried to stay above it all.

He steadfastly refused to give interviews. Even to his local paper. He asked the world's media to please get the hell off his lawn as they were trampling his tulips. Fourteen lawyers called, begging to represent him. It was bedlam. And it was destined to get so much worse as fight night grew closer. As for the change of venue, Paul refused to even consider it.

"Bloody circus," he said and slammed the front door on them.

Repeatedly.

With nobody left to talk to at the Millers' house, the media trampled the neighbours' tulips. Suddenly, everyone had an opinion. No matter how daft an opinion it was, someone with a camera and a boom mike was prepared to record it. They stalked the folks of Okotoks on every corner. You couldn't move without tripping over the media. Both motels were overbooked. Rooms in private homes were fetching outrageous prices. Vacant homes were being rented for staggering profits. And still they came. Busloads, every day. The fight was being broadcast live to seventeen cinema screens in and around Calgary. Negotiations were underway to add eleven more.

I didn't realize we had that many cinema screens in Calgary.

It was relentless. Every night, on the news, they would trot out new, self-proclaimed fight "experts" or "character witnesses." Like the guy who claimed he attended kindergarten with Paul Miller. Anyone with half a brain could see he was fifteen years younger than Paul. No matter. There was airtime to fill, and fill it they did. Everyone in Okotoks could have their fifteen minutes of fame.

If that was what they wanted.

With three days to go, I met again with Nosher and Splosher, who had been hanging around Workouts, where Adam was training Victor Shriver. Victor had missed more sessions than they'd had booked, at least until the media showed up, but it seemed of little consequence. He knew how to scrap and would be a formidable opponent regardless. There were clips of him knocking over sparring partners on every news station.

The oddsmakers were having a field day.

We had finalized Paul Miller's team about a month before the fight. Bert would be his ring coach and Bert's younger brother, Syd, would be his cut man.

When Valerie Miller learned her husband would need a cut man, the fight was almost over right then and there. We took her aside and explained that all boxers need a cut man. Even Vic Shriver needed one. Though no one expected him to get hit hard enough to bleed. Not that we told that to Valerie. She calmed down a little, complained she needed a cigarette, then popped a mouthful of peppermints instead, and we pretty much left her alone for the rest of the day.

Nosher, Splosher, Danny, Val and Cindy made up Paul Miller's cheering section. Val hadn't decided yet if she would allow her grown children to attend. With only three days remaining, they were pressuring her to make up her mind. They very much wanted to be there to cheer on their dad.

Money was discussed. Paul wanted nothing to do with it. Val took over the contract negotiations with Boss Hog at Workouts. It seemed like Paul had been a little hasty. The Pay Per View contract alone was worth five figures to the Millers.

If Paul won.

The tickets had all been sold. New tickets were printed. The new prices were suitably outrageous. Old tickets would be swapped for new tickets and the old tickets would be credited at double the face value against the new ones. Or a face-value cash refund would be given.

Or sue us.

Who cares?

The day of the fight was bedlam. Scalpers were asking, and getting, up to a grand a ticket. Boss Hog had sent four of his flunkies outside to take care of the scalpers. Two of the scalpers had escaped over the footbridge that crosses the Sheep River down near the library. The third wasn't so lucky. No one was saying whether he jumped from the bridge or if he was thrown, but the landing put him in hospital with a broken ankle. Still, they piped the fight, live, right into his room for him.

If something good came out of all the pre-publicity, it was the job offers that came Paul's way. Seven of them so far, all wanting Paul to personally handle their company advertising and promotions, and the dollars being offered, win, lose or draw, were nothing short of breathtaking.

Two hours before the fight was scheduled to start, the whole support team sat around Paul and Valerie Miller's kitchen. Val had folded and agreed the kids could come and support their father.

"If he still wants to go through with it," was her only condition.

Paul was sitting quietly on a kitchen chair. He looked each of us in the eye before finally confronting his wife.

"Your call," he said.

The room fell quiet.

She stared at him, acutely aware she held everyone's attention.

"Bastard."

Chapter Thirty-Three

PARKING WAS IMPOSSIBLE. We crowded into three cars, including Nosher and Splosher, who drove themselves. We prowled past the front of the gym. I counted at least a dozen camera crews working the crowd, seeking ever more opinions as to the outcome.

Win or lose.

That was it.

Or so I thought.

I was about to be proven wrong.

Yet again.

I was riding with Danny, Bert and Paul Miller. Danny dropped the three of us around back, at the service entrance. He wished Paul all the luck. We scurried through the back door, down a corridor to the changing room that had been allocated to us. On the way, we passed Victor Shriver's dressing room. It had a full-colour picture of Victor taped to the door, looking like he'd already won the damned fight. In the photo, he wore boxing trunks and sparring gloves, leaning forward, smiling at the camera.

There were balloons and streamers hanging from his ceiling, visible through the open door. I saw a massage table in the centre of the room and a dozen people milling around, trying hard to look important.

Paul's room was down at the end of the corridor. It might have been a closet in a previous life. Someone had thoughtfully scribbled MILLER on a piece of cardboard and taped it to the door.

No balloons. No streamers. There was no massage table, for the simple reason there wasn't room. There was a broom closet where Paul could hang his things.

Except it was full of brooms.

"Excuse me a moment," I said and excused myself.

I don't often get mad. It's a waste of an emotion. It clouds your judgment.

And you just end up hitting somebody.

So be it.

I found Boss Hog on the main floor. It was crowded with noisy fight fans and other self-important people from the world's media, all there for the taste of blood. He was wearing his gym clothes, a sprayed-on muscle shirt and Lycra tights.

Had he no shame?

The smell of popcorn, hot dogs and hamburgers wafted through the throng. Hog surrounded himself with half a dozen 'roid monkeys, not one of them under six-two and all weighing over two hundred and fifty pounds. He pretended not to notice me until I took hold of his upper arm, just above the elbow, and squeezed hard. I got his undivided attention and brought tears to his eyes.

"Goddamn it!"

He tried to shake free but I hung in there like a bulldog and smiled at him the whole time because one never knew where the cameras were.

"Smile," I told him, dragging him free of his entourage. "You're on *Candid Camera*."

"Take your fucking hands off me," he hissed.

I let him go, and he rubbed his arm fiercely.

"What the hell do you want?"

"A change of venue," I told him. "For Mr. Miller. I think the broom closet is a little beneath even you."

"Fuck you!" he snarled and put his face hard in mine, curling his lip like a feral dog in heat.

"You don't want to do that," I told him. "Not here. Not now. Not ever."

A nerve near his right eye jumped as he fought to regain control. The sudden change in atmosphere crackled through the mass of hired muscle, and they moved over and crowded me, looking to Boss Hog for direction.

"Joke's over," I said.

"That's all the room there is," he snarled. "It's all you deserve."

"Then you'd better call a press conference, tell them the fight's off." I paused, gauging his reaction. "Unless you want to go three rounds yourself."

He looked incredulous. That I could walk into his gym, that I had the effrontery to challenge him, to embarrass him in front of his troops, was simply inconceivable. His bottled-up fury left him shaking.

"One fucking word from me and any one of these

guys'll throw you head first through that fucking plate glass window." ·

"Really? Which guy?"

"Any guy."

"Pick one."

"What?"

"Pick one that can throw me through a window."

"Don't think I won't."

"Chickenshit."

He glared at me and rose to the bait.

"Russell." He nodded to the biggest, a redheaded kid with hands like meat cleavers. "Throw this asshole out."

I figured he'd pick the biggest, so I was ready for him. Russell stepped forward, meat cleavers at shoulder height. I'm not sure what he expected me to do, but hitting him really hard on the bridge of his nose with the heel of my left hand probably wasn't it.

He yowled very loudly, stopped in his tracks, grabbed at his nose but was way too late to stop the spray of blood. He staggered backwards, falling hard on his fat ass in an upright sitting position. Nobody moved for several seconds.

Except those closest to him, who scurried back, not wanting to get splattered with blood from his broken nose.

Then everyone wanted a look-see, and the lobby filled with lights, cameras, action.

"Jee-sus." Boss Hog blinked quietly in awe.

"You're next," I told him.

His demeanor quickly changed.

"He can have the room next to Vic's."

"Show him."

"What?"

"It's your gym. Go down there and make him feel welcome."

He nodded. As he turned to leave, he suddenly remembered poor Russell. He spoke to the other 'roid monkeys.

"Get him the fuck out of here."

~

The new, improved accommodations did much to alter the mood. Our changing room was the same size as Shriver's, with the addition of a shiny tampon machine. So I guess we were in the ladies' changing room. Syd the cut man, Bert's brother, checked Paul over and pronounced him fit to fight. It turned out that Syd possessed some quirky medical qualification, garnered, no doubt, from the Internet, but Bert assured me he knew what he was doing. There was a real doctor on his way, and when he arrived he gave Paul a cursory checkup before concurring with Syd's diagnosis. Syd kept his cut cream in an old Vaseline jar. When I asked him what was in it, he said it was a family secret. If I had to guess, I'd say it had copious amounts of analgesic, blood clotting agents and more than a little cocaine to take the sting out.

As long as it stemmed the blood flow.

Nosher and Splosher stopped by and wished us all well. They were ringside, but across the ring from where Val and Cindy were sitting. They promised Paul that, should he lose, Victor Shriver wouldn't walk away unscathed.

Never mind unscathed.

Their message, clearly, was that if Paul lost, Victor Shriver wouldn't walk.

Period.

I checked my watch. The fight was scheduled to start at seven-thirty. It was ten minutes before seven. Coach Bert worked on warming Paul up slowly. He didn't want to tire him out before he stepped into the ring. Danny had offered to massage Paul's neck, arms and shoulders and was busy digging his thumbs into tight muscle cells. I felt redundant to the cause and slipped away again.

I found Cindy and Val Miller in the upper level. They had ringside seats, as I'd promised. I sat next to them in an unoccupied chair. The gym was filling up quickly. The ring looked like something out of a Barnum and Bailey circus. There were bunches of red, white and blue helium-filled balloons floating above each corner post, and red, white and blue bunting was wound around the top rope on all four sides of the gym. People were selling programs for ten dollars. A lot of people in the audience were wearing buttons showing Victor's face. I figured Boss Hog was running a book and the odds-on favourite wasn't Paul Miller.

"How's he doing, Eddie?" Val asked.

"He's fine," I said. "They are warming him up slowly. Danny's working on his shoulders, keeping his muscles relaxed. He's as ready as he'll ever be."

"I keep getting cameras shoved in my face," she said.

I'd heard estimates that up to twenty-five million pay-per-view and Internet viewers were tuned to tonight's fight.

But that was just hearsay.

It could just as easily be two hundred and fifty million.

I left the girls and moved slowly around the gym. In truth, I felt I hadn't really worked hard enough to stop this fight. There had to be something I'd overlooked, something easier than having Paul go three rounds in this circus. But if there was, I was at a loss. We'd prepped him as best we could, given the time constraints and given Paul's age, both of which were working against us.

I could only pray for a miracle.

They began piping Shriver's music in just ten minutes before the fight was due to start.

Large black speakers, hanging from the ceiling, played "Street Fighting Man" against the swelling roar of the crowd. The minute hand on the wall clock moved ever closer to seven-thirty.

Somebody poked me in the shoulder. It was Gary Vaughan, the undercover cop. He was sitting two rows back, with a brassy blonde hanging off his arm.

"I've got a C-note on your guy to win," he said.

"Only bet what you can afford to lose," I said.

"Now you tell me."

There was a carnival atmosphere growing around us.

The wall clock showed seven twenty-five by the time I circulated back to Cindy and Val.

"I'd better be getting back," I told them.

I gave Cindy a hug.

Val Miller stood up, and in a move that surprised us both, she kissed me on the cheek.

"Wish him luck," she said.

I left her then, sitting in her front-row seat with her grown family next to her, worried sick, wondering what the next half hour had in store for her and for them.

As I made my way back downstairs to the Miller team

changing room, I was wondering much the same myself.

Moments later, one of Boss Hog's minions stuck his head around the door.

"You're up," he said to the room in general.

"Anybody know the protocol?" I asked.

Normally, the reigning champion arrives in the ring last. Since there was no reigning champion, we were winging it.

"Ah, they'll keep Shriver back, make some sort of grand fuckin' entrance," Bert said. "Maybe lower him from the roof in a fiery fuckin' chariot."

He draped a white cotton dressing gown over Paul's shoulders, checked his gloves one last time and tossed me his headgear.

Then the five of us walked out of the ladies' changing room into a barrage of flashbulbs, television cameras and boom mikes.

Paul Miller managed to look nonplussed.

Which was more than I could say for the rest of his crew.

Chapter Thirty-Four

THEY KEPT US WAITING IN the ring for nine long minutes, milking it for all it was worth. It was only when Bert held the ropes open and Paul ducked under that they relented and rolled out Victor Shriver. The lights dimmed, and some clown turned up the stereo.

The theme from *Rocky* blasted out.

Who'd have guessed?

Victor Shriver, along with an entourage of around twenty guys, ran up the stairs like a phalanx of Roman soldiers.

It couldn't have been cheesier had Kraft orchestrated it themselves.

Shriver wore a crimson hooded robe that scraped the floor. I hoped the son of a bitch would trip up the stairs. The back of his robe was embroidered with the name of a local car dealership. His entourage wore black hoodies, each one advertising a different sponsor. There was everything from a tanning salon to a tow-truck service.

Heading up the entourage were three bikini-clad ring girls, each carrying a board indicating the round number, in case the audience was unable to count that high. Based on the wolf whistles and catcalls, it probably wasn't a bad idea.

The referee, whom we'd been assured, repeatedly, was impartial, arrived in the midst of this throng, wearing an ill-fitting pale blue tuxedo with a frilly yellow shirt and a black bow tie. He looked like an orangutan on an acid trip.

Shriver shadowboxed his way to the front. He high-fived a variety of people in the audience, obvious plants because he clearly had no idea who they were and several times high-fived the wrong person. The cameras caught all the action, and the play-by-play commentators for Pay Per View sat at the judges' table handing out their business cards and signing autographs.

Paul managed to look bored by it all, but I'm sure it had the desired effect of unsettling him. Danny and I stayed in the ring with him until Shriver arrived. We had bar stools beside the ring, not that we expected to spend much time sitting down.

Roy Shriver climbed in and held the ropes wide apart for his son. That was to make sure Victor got his head in without a problem. While Victor continued his premature victory dance, Roy Shriver glanced across the ring. He held my eye. Then he raised his right hand, cocked his thumb and pretended to shoot me.

Again.

As we turned to go, Danny tapped Paul on the shoulder.

"If it all gets too much," he said, "kick him in the balls."

"I might do that anyway," Paul said.

We climbed out just as another orangutan, this one in a pale yellow tuxedo, climbed into the ring holding a cordless microphone. He introduced himself as Dave the Rave, your MC for the evening, and a few of the less-inhibited audience members yelled for him to shut the fuck up and to get on with it.

Dave the Rave ignored them and introduced the boxers.

"In the blue corner —" he pointed to Paul, sitting quietly on his three-legged stool "— the underdog at seventeen-to-one odds and weighing in at one hundred and eighty-two pounds, we give you Paul the Menace Miller!"

Val jumped up and began shrieking his name loudly, over and over again. To the chagrin and total embarrassment of her children, both of whom grabbed her by the arms and pulled her down into her chair. Every camera in the place moved in for a close-up.

"And in the red corner," Dave the Rave continued, moving over to Victor Shriver's corner, "we have tonight's odds-on favourite, weighing in at one hundred and seventy-seven pounds, the man who eats sparring partners for breakfast —" he paused for the crowd's reaction "— ladies and gentlemen, I give you the one, the only, the one and only, Victor Victorious Shriver!"

The elated crowd erupted. At least the fifty or so who'd been paid to attend and to put on a show. But it was contagious, and soon fifty swelled to seventy-five, then a hundred, then soon it was almost unanimous, and anything else Dave the Rave had to say was lost in a sea of rising voices and stamping feet. Cameras swung out over people's heads, sound techies ran boom mikes deep into the yelling masses, and around the globe, fight fans cracked open another round of cold beer and dug deeper into the popcorn bowl.

Let the games begin.

With Shriver were his father, of course, Adam the trainer, Boss Hog and some of Hog's steroidal pals. As the music swelled to its crescendo finish, Victor picked his moment and, in an obviously much-rehearsed move, he threw off his floor-length robe and flexed for the cameras like a prizefighter of old.

His body gleamed, an endorsement to the virtues of the tanning salon. He had little body fat, and his oiled muscles glistened under the additional lights needed for the tele-cast. He danced a tight little number, shadowboxing around his corner, pretending to chase his seconds out of the ring. Boss Hog held the rope to ensure he was the last to leave. He turned to Victor and they touched knuckles. Still not finished, Boss Hog did a double-fisted thump to his chest, then to his heart and then to his lips as he blew the crowd his sincere love and affection. The crowd was indifferent, but nonetheless Boss Hog relished his moment in the limelight.

"You fuckin' twat!" Bert saw no reason to keep his voice down, and he probably mirrored the sentiments of half the audience.

Maybe all of them.

Danny leaned over.

"Can I get one round with *him* afterwards?"

"Take a number," I said.

"That figures."

Chapter Thirty-Five

DAVE THE RAVE INTRODUCED "your referee for this evening" as Garth Wilson before bowing gracelessly out of the ring, but not before bidding Victor the best of luck.

Garth Wilson waited while someone handed him the microphone. When the audience grew a decibel or two quieter, he explained that the fight was to last three rounds, and each round was to last two minutes. Queensberry Rules would apply, and the fight was being scored under the rules of amateur boxing, which meant each fighter was awarded points for blows struck only with the white stripe that ran around the knuckle of their boxing gloves. There was to be a mandatory eight count in the event of a knockdown, during which time the remaining boxer must return to his corner.

He called both boxers to the middle of the ring and inspected their gloves, headgear, shorts and boots. When he was satisfied neither boxer had secreted a horseshoe inside a glove or down a jockstrap, he made them touch gloves, told them to keep all blows above the belt and to have a clean fight.

Then he sent them back to their respective corners, told them to come out fighting and signalled to the bellman to sound the bell for Round One.

The bell sounded loud and clear, and Victor practically ran across the ring and punched Paul in the side of the head almost before Paul had turned around.

The crowd roared, which caught Victor by surprise, and he looked out over the ropes to make sure it was him for whom they were cheering. Paul came at him, mad because he felt the fight hadn't gotten off to a fair start. He swung wildly, missed Victor's midsection but then came in close and slammed him in the ribs with a left hook. Victor backed away, looking surprised that Paul had that sort of speed and power.

They spent the next thirty seconds sparring at a distance, much to the crowd's displeasure. But it was clear that Shriver was the better boxer, and Paul was beginning to flag, breathing hard through his mouth before the round was a quarter over.

Most people have little idea just how hard a boxer really works. Not even multimillion-dollar NHL hockey players put in the full two minutes an amateur boxer endures. Or three minutes, if he's a pro. Most pro hockey lines stay out about half a minute, maybe a minute if they can't make a line change. For a boxer to go the distance, and to dish out and take a severe beating, requires an incredible amount of stamina.

Clearly, Shriver had it in spades.

During the second half of Round One, he put his stamina to good use. He switched from out-fighting, using his jab and cross punch to score points, to in-fighting, using hooks and uppercuts to hammer Paul's body hard and fast.

In the clinches, Shriver showed he knew a few dirty tricks. He hooked Paul in the liver and kidneys several times. Just before the bell, in close, after racking up a kidney shot the referee didn't notice, Victor swung a left hook at Paul's head, which Paul managed to avoid. They grappled together. With the referee on the far side, Victor was poised perfectly to head-butt Paul before the bell. As he brought his head back, Paul jabbed his thumb into Victor's unprotected eye.

Not hard.

Just hard enough to let Shriver know that one dirty trick deserved another.

The bell sounded at the end of Round One. I checked my stopwatch. It was bang on two minutes, so no cheating there.

The ref had a word with Paul as he walked him back to his corner. He knew what had just happened, and Paul looked suitably chastised. As the referee turned away, Paul looked at Victor Shriver, and the smirk on Paul's face said it all.

Shriver was rattled. He'd clearly won the first round, but Paul had surprised him with the eye poke. He'd sent Shriver a message: *Any more Mexican hooks and I'll fight fire with fire.*

Round Two promised to be a lot more interesting than Round One.

Bert and Syd worked on Paul in his corner. Shriver had

opened a quarter-inch cut above Paul's left eye, but it wasn't much of a concern unless he continued working on it, opening it up into something more serious. Syd jammed his magic elixir into the cut, and I could smell the astringent from where I was standing. I heard Paul suck in air, and I knew how it felt.

The crowd roared its approval as the second bikini-clad girl climbed into the ring, swinging her hips in an exaggerated roll as she waved the ROUND TWO card high above her head.

The bell sounded as she stepped down.

Victor wasn't so fast out of his corner the second time.

Paul took the initiative and charged across the ring towards him. Victor put up his gloves, and Paul used his weight and upper body strength to drive Victor backwards into the ropes, jamming him into the corner. He got five good body shots into Victor's ribs and solar plexus, and at least two of them really stung. Stunned, Victor pushed off from the ropes and ducked beneath Paul, moving sideways, back on the attack with a series of jabs and crosses that caught Paul off balance. He tripped and fell to his knees, and Victor came at him, crowding him, his fists high as though to deliver a crushing blow to the back of Paul's exposed neck. In defense, Paul rolled onto his back and kicked Victor, catching him just below the knee. He hooked his other foot behind Victor's leg and tripped him. Victor fell backwards, landing hard, and all the while the ref was blowing his whistle and waving his arms wildly. He pointed to the timekeeper, ordering him to stop the clock.

I didn't know the ref could do that.

When the boxers were back on their feet, he chastised them. It was hard to hear what he was saying above the yells and boos of the crowd, but both men stood like schoolboys caught smoking in the boy's room. The ref restarted the clock, insisting they touch gloves in a sportsmanlike fashion, and told them to continue fighting.

While it wasn't toe-to-toe, it had its moments. I was told that Pay Per View was charging ten bucks to watch the fight. All in all, I'd say they were getting their money's worth.

Paul scored a series of points when Victor got cocky and tried an open-handed slap. It worked the first time. Buoyed by his initial success, Victor tried it again. When he stepped forward to slap Paul's face the second time, Paul saw it coming and pummelled Victor with a series of hooks and an uppercut that almost put Victor on his ass.

By the middle of Round Two, I could see Paul was flagging. Badly. His legs were like lead, and he had stopped even trying to shift his weight from one foot to the other. He took up a stance in the middle of the ring, waited until Shriver came within range, and then switched from southpaw to right-handed.

For the first one-and-a-half rounds, he'd been fighting southpaw — leading with his right foot and hitting hardest with his left hand. He switched his feet around, leading with his left foot and using his right foot to transfer his weight to his right hook. When I threw the TV remote to him, the first time I'd met him in his library, he'd caught it with his left hand. So I assumed he was just a southpaw.

Now I realized he was truly ambidextrous.

"You see that?" I asked Danny.

He nodded.

"I'd give my right arm to be ambidextrous," he said.

Shriver didn't like it one bit. That was twice in two months someone had suckered him with the switch. Only I'd done it the other way round, switching to southpaw. The knowledgeable few in the audience loved it and began a chant in Paul's favour.

Victor stayed outside, and Paul simply waited for him to come closer. On points, it was Paul's round so far. If Shriver wanted to win this thing, he was going to have to step it up. He was looking for an opening.

It came when Paul dropped his guard. He was beyond tired, breathing hard through his slack open mouth. Every cell in his body screamed out for oxygen instead of the lactic acid that had taken up residence, and he made a mistake.

He thought Victor was two inches closer and swung a clumsy roundhouse right hook that skimmed past Victor Shriver's chin and kept going. The force of the blow spun Paul around and exposed his right side to Shriver's barrage of hammer blows, which threatened to cave in Paul's rib cage. Paul's head went back, a cry escaped him, his legs went wobbly and he almost went down.

I'm still not sure how the hell he stayed on his feet.

But he did.

He turned to face Shriver, who was moving in close to finish him off. Paul went for the earmuff defense, both hands tight over his ears, chin on his chest, body bent forward, shoulders taking the brunt of Shriver's barrage of blows.

Just as the bell went to end Round Two, Paul dropped his outside right and ripped a savage hook that caught Victor hard on the jaw, sending him pinwheeling backwards, colliding with the ref.

It was by far Paul's best shot of either round, and it brought the crowd to their feet, yelling approval.

While Bert and Syd attended to Paul, Roy Shriver and Adam took care of Victor. There seemed to be some concern in Victor Shriver's corner. He had a problem keeping his head up. Victor's shot to the jaw had hurt him. The question was, how much? As I watched, Adam reached into his pocket and pulled out something that he kept concealed. Something small that he broke in half and stuck under Victor's nose.

Amyl nitrite.

Victor's head snapped up in a split second. Paul's blow must really have done some damage for Adam to risk using amyl nitrite. It's a vasodilator, which means it rapidly expands blood vessels and quickly reduces blood pressure. Not a good idea if you're bleeding.

Danny caught it, too.

"Poppers," he said, using the street name.

"That last hook rocked him."

"Must have." He looked at Paul's corner. "They know?"

"They will."

I climbed into the ring as Syd climbed out. I told Bert what I'd seen.

"Amyl what?" Paul looked a bit groggy himself.

"He'd bleed like a pig if you can open him up," Bert said. "Crazy fucker."

I turned to climb out. There were only seconds left before the bell.

That's when I saw her.

And I knew how this fight was destined to end.

I knew all bets were off.

I yelled to Danny, but it was too late.

She was already in position.

Chapter Thirty-Six

WHEN I HADN'T SEEN HER before the fight, I figured Ruby Shriver wasn't coming. Maybe she had no interest in the outcome of the fight.

Or maybe she stayed at home taking care of their baby.

Whatever, I was surprised to see her. She must have come in along the outer wall, well away from Victor's corner. She'd made her way down through the rows between the chairs, ducking under the spectators standing near the edge of the ring on our side. She'd been carrying her handbag in both hands.

Like it was heavy.

Which it was.

She'd reached in and pulled out the Smith & Wesson I'd last seen on top of the television in Roy Shriver's trailer. At least, I was pretty sure that was the one. She'd let her handbag drop to the floor as she brought the gun up and rested it on the bottom rope, steadying her grip with both hands, her finger on the trigger.

Which is when I saw her.

I'm fast, but I'm not as fast as a speeding bullet.

She was pulling the trigger when I yelled to Danny, and he was already turning towards her, his hand reaching out to stop her when the bullet left the gun. It travelled across the ring, on a trajectory that raised it almost six feet, hitting Roy Shriver in the head. The bullet continued on, over the heads of the audience. It gained altitude and lodged in the rafters, high above the last row of spectators, all of whom had heard the gunshot and were ducking, screaming, falling backwards over chairs and turning the chaos of a boxing match into the chaos of a live shooting gallery.

Whether she intended to reload, to shoot again, is a moot point, because Danny was on her before she could act on that thought. He covered the top of the gun with one hand and scooped his other hand under the barrel, lifting it high so it threatened only the light bulbs.

He gently removed the gun from Ruby's hand, snapped it open and emptied out the shells. He put them in his pocket and held the empty gun behind him so I could take it. He frisked Ruby quickly but thoroughly. When he was satisfied she carried no other guns, he slid her purse across the floor to me with his right foot. I searched her purse, which was empty.

There were no more guns.

But the whole place was in an uproar.

I sought out Cindy. She was comforting Valerie Miller, guiding her around the ring towards us, away from the mad scramble of bodies falling over themselves to escape the next bullet.

In the far corner, Roy Shriver lay face down on the canvas, an expanding pool of blood forming around his head. Victor seemed to be in total shock. I glanced up at Paul and Bert. They couldn't understand what was happening. I grabbed Syd's shoulder.

"Syd," I said. "Why don't you go over and see if you can help Mr. Shriver. He's the one got shot in the head."

Syd looked a bit shell-shocked himself but quickly recovered and hurried across the ring.

He was carrying his jar of cut cream.

For all the good that would do.

I found the microphone that had been tossed aside in the headlong rush. It was still on. I tried to assure everyone who would listen that the danger had passed. The gun was empty. It was in safe hands. The shooter had been subdued. But the microphone might have been turned off for all the good it did. People continued to crash about, falling on their hands and knees, scrambling to escape death by shooting. They poured down the wide staircase, ignoring the sinking-ship rule of women and children first.

It was every man for himself.

As the gym emptied, the noise level went down, and Victor Shriver came slowly across the ring to where Ruby stood, motionless in Danny's grip.

"Ruby?"

It was all he could say.

"Ruby?"

He got down on his knees at the edge of the ring.

"Was you shootin' at me?"

She didn't answer.

I spoke his name.

Finally, he turned to look at me. He tried to speak but nothing came out.

"Vic," I said again. "She's a better shot than that."

He stared at me until my words made sense to him.

"Oh, Ruby, baby." He stared at her. "What God-in-hell thing did he do to you this time?"

She looked him in the eye, but she was beyond words.

The RCMP came howling into the chaos of the parking lot, guns drawn, flattening themselves out on the staircase, yelling for everyone to get down on the floor, to throw their guns out and put their hands behind their heads.

I walked towards the stairs, my arms out by my side.

"Is Nicole Laurin with you?" I called to them.

I heard radio chatter, and someone yelled back.

"Identify yourself!"

"I'm Eddie Dancer. I'm a private investigator. We've had a single shooting. One man's down. The perp's been disarmed. I have the gun. It's empty. I will put it down near the top of the stairs when you instruct me to do so. Have you located Nicole Laurin yet? She can vouch for me."

"Identify yourself again!" the voice yelled.

"Dancer. Eddie Dancer."

I kept my voice calm. No point upsetting anyone else. The average handgun needs less than four pounds of pressure to discharge, and I figured there were probably twelve of them pointing in my direction.

"Nicole's here. She's coming up. Don't move a muscle!"

"This is me not moving."

It seemed to take forever, but eventually Nicole peered quickly over the staircase and withdrew her head just as fast.

"Hi, Nicole."

"Hi, Eddie."

"We had a situation here but everything's under control. The shooter is in my partner's custody. I have her only weapon."

"Her?"

"Yeah. It was Ruby."

"Oh, Christ."

"She shot her father-in-law."

"Is he dead?"

"No, but he may be if we don't get this done in time."

Her head popped up.

"Where's the gun?"

This time, she stayed in view. I reached over to open my jacket very, very carefully. The Smith & Wesson was jammed down the front of my pants.

"Is it empty?"

"You think I'd stash it there if it wasn't?"

A snigger.

"Okay. Take it out. Carefully."

"I know the drill."

"That's because he's an ex-cop, gentlemen." Nicole Laurin addressed her fellow officers. "It's not because he's an armed or dangerous man. That right, Eddie?"

"That's right."

I used one finger and one hand. As the gun popped free, I could hear a needle drop. I got down on my knees, probably unnecessarily but I thought it was a nice gesture, one designed to persuade them not to blow my head off. I shuffled forward, the gun swinging like a metronome from my outstretched finger on my outstretched arm. I reached the head of the stairs and tried not to look at the gun barrels pointed at my chest.

Central mass.

Aim for the biggest target.

I'm glad I have a small ass.

I laid the gun down on the floor and moved back six feet. I thought I heard a collective sigh, but that might have been wishful thinking.

Nicole stepped forward, scooped up the gun and passed it down the stairs.

Even with the gun in their possession, they came in slowly, guns still drawn, covering one another as they moved slowly forward, sweeping the entire upper gym. A man in full tactical gear took command and declared the area secure.

But he still kept his finger on the trigger and the safety off.

The paramedics came in right behind them. They wasted no time asking questions. They quickly lifted Roy Shriver onto a stretcher, cut off his shirt and ran an intravenous line into his body, then slid the stretcher off the canvas and carried him out of the gym into the waiting ambulance. I heard the *whoop, whoop, whoop* of their siren recede as they sped away.

The RCMP had Ruby in cuffs. They were very gentle with her. It was as if they had known this might happen one day.

But how could they not?

I think they thought she was aiming at Victor and had hit Roy by mistake. Everyone in our party stayed and gave statements and promised to make ourselves available if we were needed. The Mounties took Ruby away and allowed Victor to get dressed, promising him a ride to the hospital to be with his father.

I watched it all with a sense of guilt. Not for Roy Shriver. I couldn't care if he lived or died. But that Ruby took matters into her own hands was my fault. I'd seen what he'd done to her. I'd done nothing about it.

I saw Danny watching me, and I turned away. He was my closest friend but I couldn't face him right now. In fact, I couldn't face anyone.

Least of all myself.

Chapter Thirty-Seven

ROY SHRIVER LIVED.

So they charged Ruby with attempted murder. At her preliminary trial, the judge listened dispassionately to the details before ruling that Ruby undergo a psychiatric evaluation.

Which wasn't the worst of outcomes.

I'd spent time with Ruby's lawyer, Dixie Forester, a good friend who owed me a favour and whose bill I'd promised to settle on behalf of Ruby if Dixie promised not to tell her it was me. I told her what I'd seen, and Dixie said she now had several defence options and the fact that Ruby had been sexually assaulted by her father-in-law would lay heavily on the prosecution if they tried to paint Roy Shriver as anything other than a class-one scumbag.

I'd sworn Dixie to secrecy. Unless Ruby was prepared to talk about it, I forbade Dixie to speak of it either.

"Jeez, Eddie." She threw her hands in the air. "It's a rock-solid defence, fer Chrissakes."

"Find another one," I told her.

"If she refuses to admit he molested her, refuses to admit he beat her . . ."

"I never saw him beat her."

"But you have cause to think he did."

I stared at her. She was definitely one of the best-looking lawyers ever to grace a courtroom. Medium height with short-cropped blonde hair streaked through with blonde-on-blonde highlights that only a high-priced, three-figure stylist could achieve. She had prominent cheekbones and just enough of an overbite to give you whiplash as she strode by, and she wore the most stylish clothes that hugged every delicious curve, the way God intended.

"Eddie. She must have been under terrible pressure, living out there with two men who abused her regularly. The wonder of it is that she didn't kill the damned pair of them. I would. I can get her off, or at least a greatly reduced sentence, maybe even time served by the time this gets to court. It's a justifiable defence, Eddie. I don't understand why you won't let me run with it."

"Yes you do."

"Tell me again."

I sighed. She was being obtuse.

"Because it's her life. It's her choice."

She was quiet for a moment.

"Listen." She looked at me pleadingly. "I'm going to see her again tomorrow. Come with me."

"I'll think about it."

She scribbled something down on a notepad, tore it off and handed it to me.

"This is where they're keeping her. I'm seeing her at

two-thirty. If you can make it, call me by noon. I need to get you booked in. They won't let you in otherwise. Okay?"

I nodded.

I knew I should go. I knew it was the right thing to do. I got all the way down to the main floor before I turned around and took the elevator back to her office.

"Two-thirty?"

She never even looked up from her desk.

"I knew you'd change your mind."

Chapter Thirty-Eight

THE PSYCHIATRIC ASSESSMENT program was oversubscribed. They had taken temporary ownership of a residential home in Mount Royal that had fallen foul of the Proceeds of Crime rules several years earlier. I picked up Dixie from her office and drove to Mount Royal, which lies just east of downtown and features some of the most expensive homes in the city. Huge lots with massive stone-faced castles lurked behind rows of ancient pines. The house we were looking for bore no signage, no discreet brass name plate, nothing other than the street number tactfully carved from a chunk of granite that sat near an opening in the row of trees. The drive was barred to all and sundry by an electronic metal gate. I leaned over and pressed the security button built into a stone pillar.

A polite male voice spoke softly from the wall-mounted speaker.

"May I help you?"

"Dixie Forester to see Ruby Shriver," I said into the grille work.

There was a brief silence.

"Sir?"

"Yes?"

"Is Miss Forester with you?"

"Of course."

"May I speak with her, sir?"

"Sure."

Dixie undid her seat belt, leaned right across me and poked her head out the driver's window. She had a very shapely bum. I resisted the temptation to rest my hand upon it but I did give thanks to the Almighty.

"Hello?"

"Miss Forester?"

"Speaking."

"You're here to see?"

"Ruby Shriver. I'm her lawyer. I'm with Mr. Dancer." Dixie Forester turned and frowned at me, as though she'd only just realized the position she was in and the opportunity it afforded a less scrupulous person than I. "He's Mrs. Shriver's private investigator."

A metallic click was followed by a gentle hum as the gate slowly opened.

"Please tell your driver to pull all the way around back and park in visitor parking."

I watched while Dixie wriggled free. I gave her a polite round of applause and she gave me a look that would have withered a lesser man.

But not me.

"Hussy," I said.

The back lot was paved, and there was visitor and staff

parking for maybe twenty cars. It was half full. We went in through the rear entrance, where a security guard checked our IDs. He buzzed upstairs to ensure we were both expected, then handed us our security passes, which we wore around our necks.

We took the stairs to the second floor and were met by Dr. Raoul Kishman, the resident psychiatrist. He wore a three-piece wool suit with a floral bow tie.

Normally, I hate bow ties. Ergo, I hate men who wear the bloody things, but I was willing to make an exception. Dr. Kishman wore his well, as though he were aware it was passé, and he wore it more with humour than any real attempt to appear stylish. He greeted us warmly and steered us into the Day Room, according to the sign on the door.

It was a long room, fairly narrow, which made me suspect that a wall had been removed. It overflowed with chesterfields and coffee tables, and a big-screen television. The drapes were drawn and the room was lit by lamplight. The room had a warm, informal feel. We sat across from Dr. Kishman and he tried his best to concentrate on Dixie's face, and not on her legs, as she crossed them above the knee, seated on a deeply cushioned chesterfield.

Round One to Dixie.

"I'm Ruby Shriver's court-appointed doctor," Kishman said, getting right down to business. "I understand you're her lawyer?"

"Yes."

"And Mr. Dancer is . . .?"

"Mr. Dancer is a private detective," Dixie answered for me. "He has taken an interest in Ruby's situation as he believes there may be mitigating circumstances that led to her hostility."

Dr. Kishman steepled his fingers over his knees and leaned in towards me, expecting me to pick up where Dixie left off. I looked him in the eye but never said a word. The silence grew strained.

"What mitigating circumstances, Mr. Dancer?"

"Has Ruby not confided in you, Dr. Kishman?" I asked.

"She's confided many things. I'm not sure we are speaking specifically enough here."

"Unless Ruby Shriver tells me I can share the information with you or anyone else, my lips are sealed. Is that specific enough, Dr. Kishman?"

"I certainly didn't mean to pry, Mr. Dancer."

"Of course you did. That's your job. And I would think less of you if you hadn't tried. But, as I said, until Ruby tells me otherwise, everything she says to me is in the strictest confidence."

He sat back and nodded, looking very wise.

"I understand. Would you like to speak with her now?"

"We would," Dixie said.

"One question, though." I held up a finger that froze the conversation. "Will our conversations be recorded?"

"Not if you don't wish them to be."

"I think you can take it as given that both Miss Forester and I require all and any of our conversations with Ruby Shriver to remain strictly private and confidential. If any portion of such conversation should be accidentally recorded, Dr. Kishman, you personally will see to it that such recordings will be immediately erased and cannot be used against her."

236

I caught Dixie's breathless look.

"So be it," he said.

"Then, yes, I think we would like to meet with Mrs. Shriver."

As we followed Kishman upstairs to Ruby's room, Dixie looped her arm through mine and squeezed.

Ah, the fairer sex.

They're so impressionable.

Chapter Thirty-Nine

IT WAS OBVIOUS FROM the outset that Ruby had been heavily sedated. Her room was fairly small but well furnished, with a bed, a night table and two wing chairs flanking an occasional table. The drapes were pulled shut and the only light in the room came from a large floor lamp in the corner.

The wallpaper reminded me of a Victorian tea room.

The door to her room was locked, accessed via a card similar to those used by many hotels. Once we were inside, I tested the door. It was locked from the inside, too.

Ruby lay on her bed, wearing a housecoat over a T-shirt and jeans. Her feet were bare, her toenails in need of a fresh coat of paint. Her hair was dull, her eyes fixed and glazed like overcooked ham.

"Dr. Kishman?"

He turned to me, lifted his chin in response.

"Can you give her something to make her more comfortable?"

"Comfortable?"

"Frankly, Doc, she looks like a goddamn zombie. Can

you give her something to counter the effects of whatever you've doped her with? We need to talk with her. We need her alert. We can't help her at all while she's in this state."

He turned and looked at her, checked her pulse, lifted her eyelids, peered into her eyes with a flashlight as thin as a pencil. He looked at his watch and then promised he'd be right back.

We sat and stared at her and I doubt she even knew who we were. She was breathing, but that was about it.

Kishman was back five minutes later. He had a thin syringe full of something colourless, and I looked away when he poked the needle into Ruby's arm.

Sorry, Ruby.

I hate needles.

I assume everyone else does.

It took about ten minutes to bring Ruby back from the land of the living dead. She let out a deep shudder and rubbed her arms as though she were cold.

"Ruby?"

Kishman sat next to her on the bed. She turned her head towards him and blinked, as if waking from a deep sleep. She frowned at him.

"You have visitors, Ruby."

She looked up, and Dixie wiggled her fingers by way of a wave. I smiled, but she didn't respond.

"I'm going to leave you alone with your visitors now, Ruby. If you want anything, anything at all, you know where the call button is?"

Ruby reached over and touched a red button pinned to the edge of her bedsheet.

"Good. Is there anything you need for now?"

She shook her head, then changed her mind.

"Coffee," she said, her voice hoarse.

"I'll send Maxine up with coffee for everyone."

He left us then and I heard the lock click shut behind him. I looked for evidence of a hidden camera but couldn't see any.

I let Dixie start.

"Ruby?" Ruby looked over. "How are you feeling?"

It took her a while before she answered.

"Okay. A bit groggy."

"Are you okay to talk?"

"Yeah."

"You know Eddie Dancer, yes?"

She looked at me then, and she nodded warily, not bothering to speak.

"Mr. Dancer believes you had good reason to do what you did."

She didn't answer.

"He wants you to give him permission to tell the courts."

She frowned.

"Does that surprise you, Ruby?" she said.

Again, the long wait before she answered.

"Why does he want to tell them?" she asked.

"Because he wants to help you."

She looked at me as if she didn't believe a thing I might say.

"He saw something that could be important. That could help the judge decide how your trial will go. You do want help, don't you?"

While she was thinking about it, the door opened and a woman came in carrying a tray of coffee.

"Hello." She smiled warmly at us. She had included a plate of assorted cookies. "I've put in some of the dark chocolate ones you like, Ruby."

Ruby nodded and the woman left, locking the door behind her. I let Dixie pour the coffee and helped myself to sugar and a whole-wheat cookie. Then Dixie continued coaxing Ruby.

It was like talking to a child standing at the edge of a cliff.

"Ruby? You do want help, don't you?"

"I guess."

"So will you give your blessing?"

"My blessing?"

"Will you allow Mr. Dancer to say what he saw?"

"I don't know."

Dixie seemed to fold. She didn't have a lot of experience with the Rubys of this world. But she was a good lawyer. I stood up, put my coffee aside and walked over to Ruby. I sat on the edge of her bed and stared down at her, waiting for her to acknowledge me.

It took a while, but finally she looked at me.

"Ruby," I said. "I know you don't like me. I wouldn't like me either, if I was you. I tricked you. I wasn't honest with you. For those things, I'm sorry. I truly am."

She watched me the way you'd watch a dangerous animal, ready to turn and run the moment it moved closer.

I tried again.

"Because of that, because of the way I treated you, I've

come to understand you a little better. I've come to understand what you live with. And that's put me in a position where I can help you. Where I can do you some good." I waited, but if she was thinking of changing her mind, she wasn't about to show it. "Can I make a suggestion?"

She didn't say anything but I saw her head move, maybe a millimetre.

I took that as a nod.

"Can we start again? Can we start from scratch?"

Another tiny movement.

Another millimetre of assent.

"I have seen a lot of women in your position. Women whose husbands beat them, who live in fear, every day of their lives."

She moved her head again. But this time it went the other way. She shook it, not a nod. Disagreeing with me.

I thought about what I'd said.

"It wasn't Victor?"

Another tiny shake.

"It was Roy?"

A nod.

"Not all the time?"

A shake.

"Most of the time?"

A nod. "Yes." A tiny sound.

"What's going on?" Dixie wanted in on this.

"Can I tell her?"

Ruby looked so damned scared, so alone, so small and pitiful. I reached out to her, put my hand against her cheek. I saw her flinch, saw the sudden fear that narrowed her eyes and pinched the skin on her face, made the muscles twitch beneath my palm. But I kept my hand on her cheek, rubbed her jawline softly with my thumb until she began to adjust, began to soften, to release the fear.

Finally, she reached up and placed her own hand on top of mine. She let it rest there and held my hand against her cheek for a long time. Finally, she nodded her head and I told Dixie what I'd seen, how Roy Shriver had sexually assaulted her out in the open.

I felt Ruby's tears, hot liquid in my open palm. She cried quietly as she finally broke down. She told us of the many times Roy had raped her when Victor was away. If she tried to fight him off, he'd beaten her, broken her bones, threatened to kill her if she told a living soul. She lived in fear of her life.

I felt ashamed to be a man. Ashamed that another man had reduced this shy, beautiful creature to something so much less than she could have been. My shame escaped me and ran down my cheeks in its haste to run away.

I tasted salt.

Then Ruby slid her hand around the back of my neck and, shaking, lifted herself up, burying her head against my neck and wailing, years of tears, a lifetime of neglect suddenly erupting into an emotion so intense, it took her breath away and she panted, gasping for breath between her gut-wracking sobs.

I held her close and told her, again and again, how sorry I was.

When she finally stopped crying, Dixie found a box of tissue and wiped Ruby's face. Then, with cosmetics from her own purse, she repaired the damage to Ruby's face. She powdered her, applied eyeliner and lipstick, held the mirror to show Ruby the progress she was making.

Finally, we talked about Victor. She admitted Victor had hit her, but not often and he was always contrite for days afterwards. She was still in denial, believing he had his reasons and that she deserved to be hit.

When we asked why Victor Shriver never confronted his father, all she would say was that Victor was scared of him.

But why was he so scared of his father? Why had he refused to stand up to him?

"Because of something terrible his father had done. Years ago."

Again, she fell silent.

I asked her what terrible thing Roy Shriver had done.

She began crying again, smudging the makeup Dixie had applied.

"I can't tell you," was all she said.

Chapter Forty

DIXIE WANTED TO GET MY deposition on tape as soon as we left Mount Royal. I agreed to drive her back to her office and finish up there. I pulled away from the Mount Royal house and was about to turn left, back downtown, when I stopped. A rusty brown Ford Granada drove past us, heading in the opposite direction. I recognized Victor Shriver at the wheel. I watched him in my mirror as he pulled up to the same metal gate.

"Does her husband have access?" I asked Dixie.

"Unfortunately," she replied.

The heavy metal gate swung open and Victor Shriver drove in to see his wife.

"There ain't no justice," I told Dixie.

"That's why we have lawyers," she said.

I tried not to snort.

~

Her downtown office offered views of the mountains, if you stood on the filing cabinet and leaned over at a sixty-degree angle. Otherwise, you had to content yourself with a view of the railway tracks heading west. When she said she wanted to tape my deposition, she meant videotape. She sat me before a tripod-mounted camera, told me to look into the lens and speak clearly. She gave me a three count and said, "Go."

I stated my name, occupation and the date and time, then I launched into a detailed explanation of how I came to witness the sexual molestation of one Ruby Shriver by her father-in-law, Roy Shriver. When I tried to explain why I didn't intercede, Dixie waved me off. She told me it was irrelevant. She said she'd edit that bit out anyway. I just felt that it was important the judge understand I wasn't a total jerk.

"He won't have an opinion one way or the other, Eddie. This is simply to help build a credible case of justifiability on Ruby's part."

After we'd finished, Dixie thanked me and offered to buy lunch. I said I'd take a rain check. I didn't think I'd be very good company.

I drove to my office and sat behind the desk, put my feet up and wondered what to do next. I couldn't think of anything, so I waited for my phone to ring. But phones are like watched kettles and they won't ring, nor will they boil, if you're watching them. Finally, bored with my own company and my inability to move forward, I decided to grab a snooze. I kicked off my shoes and hunkered down at my desk to wait for sleep to overtake me. No sooner did it, than my phone rang.

My unwatched phone.

It was Valerie Miller. She was phoning to let me know the outcome of the fight. At least, in the opinion of the ringside judges, even though I'd already given it to Ruby.

It was, according to the judges, a draw.

Which meant that Paul and Victor shared the pot, a sizeable windfall. On top of that, the fight had generated an enormous amount of publicity that had now translated into fourteen serious job offers for Paul Miller. Three major advertising agencies were clamouring for his attention and the salaries being discussed were outrageous.

Paul felt vindicated, finally, and Val thanked me, promising me an invite to the upcoming party to celebrate their newfound notoriety. She was planning something with a boxing theme. Paul had agreed to foot the bill.

I spent the next day with Danny, at his Eau Claire condo, which looked down on Calgarians the size of ants and cars the size of sugar cubes. We talked about our feelings towards Victor and towards his father.

We agreed we couldn't rest on our laurels where Roy Shriver was concerned. We needed retribution.

As it turned out, the gods were already moving the scenery around to everyone's benefit.

Except Roy Shriver's.

Chapter Forty-One

THE REST OF THE WEEK passed slowly. My phone hardly rang. The hookers on Eleventh Avenue got younger and the johns got older. The kid in the studio next door was scoring a major movie, and every so often, the walls reverberated to the futuristic soundtrack. I wondered if he'd maybe invite me over to watch it with him.

On Friday morning my phone rang with news.

"Hello?"

It was Dr. Kishman.

He of the dickie-bow.

He told me that Ruby had asked if I could come and see her.

This morning.

Right now, in fact.

It was important.

I was driving through the main gate less than fifteen minutes after taking his call. The hell with visitor's parking. I parked in front and took the stairs four at a time.

I was surprised to see Victor Shriver in Ruby's room.

The room was dark. The drapes were pulled shut. I waited a few seconds for my eyes to adjust. Ruby was sitting in one of the wing chairs, ramrod straight. Victor lay huddled on her bed.

"Good morning." She spoke quietly, her voice ragged and worn around the edges.

"Good morning, Ruby."

I stayed put, waiting for her to continue.

"Would you like to sit?"

I sat down.

"Has Victor been here all night?"

"Yes."

"Which probably has something to do with why I'm here?"

"Yes." She took a deep breath and spoke slowly. "I've always known he had a secret," she said. "I told you that. I told you it was something terrible, something that scared him to even think about. Well, last night, this morning, he told me what that terrible thing was."

I held my breath.

"I think the timing is important," she said.

Timing?

"That his father will live," she said.

The timing?

"I'm not following you, Ruby."

"If his father had died, I doubt he would have told me."

"Okay."

"But he didn't die. He lived. And now Victor has to relive the same nightmare, all over again."

"Ruby. Tell me what he did."

And, although I wasn't there, this is what happened to Victor Shriver when he was six years old, living on the acreage east of the overpass with his younger sister, Bethany, as told to me by Ruby Shriver, Victor's wife of eleven years.

Chapter Forty-Two

VICTOR AND BETHANY WERE playing in the makeshift sand-box alongside their parents' trailer early that warm summer's morning. It was, he thinks, a Sunday, because his father was home, sleeping in. The day was already warm. Their mother was indoors, nursing another of her never-ending headaches, sipping medicine from a small brown bottle. Victor remembered her breath always smelled of oranges. He wondered, many years later, if she were sipping morphine, because liquid morphine can smell like tangerines.

The two children played well together. They had much in common, not the least of which was the beatings regularly inflicted upon them by their father. Their mother rarely interfered with these punishments and offered little in the way of comfort in their aftermath. But to be fair, she was just as likely to be the recipient of such beatings as they were.

On this particular day, they were playing quietly, building sandcastles, using a couple of old jam jars. Little Victor would fill them with sand and Bethany would flip them over, pat the top with the sandbox spade and lift the jar carefully, leaving behind a perfect imprint of the jar's insides. They had built a row of ten or twelve little towers when Bethany gave the jar an overenthusiastic whack. The jar broke, falling apart in the sand.

Bethany was mad. She whacked the sandcastle with the spade, sending sand in all directions, then she stood up and kicked the broken jam jar.

Which was the wrong thing to do, because she was barefoot.

The blood sprayed out in a fine arc over Victor's shoulder. As soon as Bethany saw the blood and realized it was hers, she began to cry. Afraid she would wake their father, and fearful of the consequences, Victor picked her up, trying to console her.

But Bethany would not be consoled.

The sight of her own blood struck fear in her, and she began screaming. Loud, incessant, piercing screams that travelled through the metal walls and the thin insulation of the trailer, burrowing deeply into their father's sleeping brain.

Within moments, the trailer door flew open.

Roy Shriver, his face puffy with broken sleep and lined with pillow ridges, stood in the sunlight and bellowed at them to shut the fuck up.

Which only made Bethany worse.

He came down off the deck and grabbed her by the arm, shook her until she was just a blur. Blood from her cut foot sprayed across Roy's feet, which seemed to incense him further. He threw her in the dirt and towered above them both, breathing like a bull filled with blood lust.

"You've goddamn well asked for it this time," he hissed.

Victor knew what the punishment would be.

And he wet himself.

He pleaded with his father not to do it. He promised, over and over, to be good. He promised never, ever to make another sound as long as he lived. And he promised the same of Bethany, who lay sobbing in the dirt.

But to no avail.

Before Victor was born, the Shrivers had a dog. It lived most of its pitiful life in a dog cage. When it died, Roy Shriver could have thrown the cage away.

But he didn't.

It was a three-by-three-by-four foot metal cage with a hinged door and a heavy carrying handle welded to the roof.

Roy Shriver had another idea for the dog cage.

The Shrivers also had a well.

It was like a wishing well, with a low stone wall supporting a thick wooden shaft, from which hung a rope attached to a wooden bucket. The dark, brackish water of the well lay thirty feet down. Victor knew this because his father used to lock him in the cage and lower him into the water. This Roy would do with some regularity; Victor could remember this punishment being visited upon him at least a dozen times.

Spare the rod, spoil the child.

And then it would be Bethany's turn.

Except this day, Roy put Bethany in first.

Victor watched, sickened, as the cage disappeared. He knew what came next. The long, terrifying journey down into icy black water. As the water poured in through the open bars, you had one last chance to take a breath, to hold your nose, to squeeze your eyes shut, to count to ten.

With every second you hoped your father wasn't counting slower than you.

Then the sudden lurch, the upward rush, the water falling away. Sensations he would never forget.

Except today was different.

Today the handle turned too freely.

Because today, the rope came up empty.

Chapter Forty-Three

I STOOD BEHIND NICOLE Laurin on Roy Shriver's front porch. Behind us, an entire SWAT team lay in the undergrowth. I was the only one not wearing body armour. Nicole pounded on the door with a fist.

"RCMP!" she bellowed. "Open up."

A curtain moved in the far bedroom. A dozen riot guns clicked as the safeties came off.

"What d'you want?"

"Roy Shriver?"

"Who's askin'?"

"RCMP. Open the door or I'll kick it in and we'll mace you!"

He elected to open the door. He looked much the same, except for the bloodstained bandage around his head. He'd effected his own discharge from the hospital two days before. It had taken a couple of days to secure the warrant to search the well and gather the equipment necessary to empty it.

Roy Shriver had filled the well with rocks the day after

he had drowned Bethany. He had worked tirelessly all day, fanning the rocks out where there had once been a low stone wall. He hadn't even bothered with a cross.

The day after Bethany died, a driller dropped a new shaft, a good distance from the old well. The new well went one hundred and sixty-five feet, straight down.

"We have a warrant to search the well," Nicole told him.

Roy looked puzzled. Clearly, he was thinking of the new well, not the old one. But when he saw the backhoe, and the tow truck with the extended jib, when he saw the men in overalls with picks and shovels, he finally understood.

He tried to shut the door.

He was fast.

I was faster.

I wedged my foot in the opening, and the door ricocheted open. I stepped inside and took Roy Shriver by the throat, single-handed. I reached back, and Nicole handed me a set of handcuffs.

"Lock him in the back of my cruiser," she said, "and I don't want to see any bruises."

I closed the door with my heel.

This time it stayed shut.

I had a choice, of course. I could have beaten him to within an inch of his life. The way I felt, I could have happily beaten him all the way to dead. Or I could have handcuffed him and put him the back of the cruiser alive.

I guess I was being tested.

So I turned him around, slammed him face-first into the wall and cuffed him, snapping the cuffs on his bony wrists really tight. I dragged him out and put him in the back of Nicole's cruiser. I especially liked the bit where I forgot to put my hand on top of his head to stop it from slamming into the edge of the roof.

Twice.

Later, at the well site, I saw Ruby watching from her trailer. Dr. Kishman had arranged for her to be there with Victor. He felt it was an important step in her defence. She was under continual police watch. I didn't go over, just sat on a rock and watched as men and machines hauled tons of rocks from the well shaft. By mid-afternoon, they reached the water. Progress slowed, and they lowered divers down, brave men who manhandled rocks into baskets and pressed themselves against the cold brick walls to avoid getting crushed as the baskets were hauled up the shaft, emptied, then dropped back down again.

I don't know when Danny arrived. He simply materialized alongside me, as only Danny can. One moment, I was alone. The next I drew comfort from his presence. He looked at me, read my face, assessed the damage, noted it all and filed it away. Then he stared at the hole and never took his eyes off it.

They found Bethany Shriver at six-fifteen that evening.

A sombre quiet went through the men and women around the hole. Hats came off. A door opened, and Ruby came out of her trailer. She helped Victor step down off the porch. I watched them move slowly across the uneven ground, Ruby in her long summer dress, Victor looking thin in jeans, his shirt hanging out. They moved closer, and armed men respectfully moved out of their way.

Before they brought Bethany up, Nicole sent two men to

bring Roy Shriver down to the well site. Everyone stopped and waited. They cuffed him to Ruby's clothesline post, and he slid down, trying to make himself small.

To make himself invisible.

The cage banged against the side of the well. It was flatter than it had been, but by some miracle, it was still intact. Inside, the bones of little Bethany Shriver lay huddled in a tiny, pathetic pile of rotted rags.

There were sobs as grown men cried.

Family men with guns.

Nicole reached out, unclipped the hook and helped lift Bethany's remains onto terra firma. She closed her eyes and made the sign of the cross.

There was a heavy stillness in the air.

Then I felt Danny move against me.

By the time I'd turned to look where he was looking, Victor was already on the move. He'd reached under his shirt and his hand came out with a gun. He moved towards Roy Shriver, who watched him coming.

"You bastard!"

It echoed around the yard.

Victor moved on his father, his arms outstretched, both hands wrapped around the gun.

The reaction was immediate. You cannot pull a gun in the company of armed men without getting the reaction Victor got. Guns came out; men ran for cover or threw themselves flat on the ground. I moved to Ruby, took her arm, tried to guide her away, but she shook me off, yelling at Victor not to shoot.

"Drop the gun!"

A man in a flack suit took command, his voice strong and forceful, yelling at Victor, who ignored him. I'm not sure Victor could hear even him, lost as he was in his fear and his rage and his awful childhood memories.

"Now! Put the gun down!"

But Victor didn't. He moved towards his father, who finally seemed to realize that the son he'd bullied for so long was to be the instrument of his execution.

There was a brief standoff.

Ruby pleaded, the policeman commanded and Roy Shriver begged for his life. We were frozen. All of us.

But not quite all.

From the corner of my eye I saw a movement, a shadow that passed between the prone and hidden bodies of armed policemen, and quickly stepped in front of Victor and slowly opened his arms.

And Victor, the beaten, abused, confused and distraught six-year-old, slowly lowered the gun, let it drop from his fingers and stepped forward, into Danny's arms.

We watched, speechless to a man, as Victor cried.

Like a lost, lonely child.

Chapter Forty-Four

I WAS LAYING IN BED NEXT to Cindy Palmer, feeling myself come to life again. She raked perfect nails across my belly. Her little finger dropped into my belly button.

She liked an innie, she said.

It was very useful when eating celery.

"Useful?" I said.

"It where you keep the salt," she said, like I was an idiot not to know that.

I wondered about a woman like that. Who eats celery with salt? The phone rang.

"Whose house are we in?" I asked.

"Yours."

"Damn."

"What?"

"I have to answer it."

"So?"

"I'll spill the salt."

"Hang on."

She disappeared a moment. I felt her warm, moist

tongue inside my belly button. She smacked her lips and reappeared.

"Go."

I got up and answered the phone. It felt nice to stand naked in my own bedroom at three in the afternoon.

"Mr. Dancer?"

I knew the voice. Images of dickie-bows floated through my brain.

"Dr. Kishman. How are you?"

Who can resist asking psychiatrists how they are? They never tell you the truth.

"I'm very well, all things considered," he replied, hedging his bets in case I was keeping score. "I thought you'd be interested in knowing how my meeting with the judge went this afternoon."

That was today? I needed to spend less time in bed.

"Absolutely."

"All charges are being dropped."

"Against Ruby?"

"Yes. Who else is there?"

Who indeed?

"What's the catch?"

"No catch. Oh, she's to attend regular sessions with me, and I've volunteered to help her husband through the worst of his situation. It behooves them to spend therapy time together."

Behooves?

"I just wanted to let you know. I understand the father has made a full confession."

"Confession is good for the soul."

"Indeed, it is. But he will be spending the rest of his days behind bars."

"How fitting."

He let that one go.

"Thank you for all your help," he said.

"You're welcome," I told him.

He was quiet for a moment. I knew he had more to say, so I waited him out.

"This friend of yours," he said.

"Which one?"

"Daniel."

"Don't ever let him hear you call him Daniel. His name is Danny."

"Danny, then. A fascinating person, I'm told."

"Isn't he."

"What can you tell me of him?"

"You know all you need to know, Doc."

"I see."

"Don't even go there," I told him. "He's a whole other branch of medicine."

"If you're sure," he said.

"I'm very sure."

"Then I'll bid you farewell."

"Likewise."

We hung up together.

"Who was that?" a muffled voice asked from under the covers.

"Doctor Doolittle."

She peered out and scrutinized me with come-to-bed eyes.

"Hey, big boy," she drawled. "Wanna dip your celery stick in my salt pot?"

And as unsavoury as that sounded, she was actually quite sweet.